Comanche Summer: Texas Ranger Days

The Ballad of Shannon Dumas - A Novella

A. K. Vyas

For Zehra and Zaynab
Godspeed

"These areas are our home, and we cannot leave them; our dead are here; our children are here."
- Chief Ten Bears of the Comanche

"I must say as to what I have seen of Texas it is the garden spot of the world. The best land and the best prospects for health I ever saw, and I do believe it is a fortune to any man to come here. There is a world of country here to settle."
- Davy Crockett

CONTENTS

PREFACE

T HIS NOVELETTE IS SET over an unforgettable summer in 1860s Comancheria when Shannon Dumas was a young Texas Ranger. It features additional characters and events from the first book of the full-length Ballad of Shannon Dumas series.

The Texas frontier was a rough, wild, dangerous place. In hindsight it's possible to empathize with both sides in a clash of civilizations. The Native American tribes were proud, fierce peoples defending their lands and way of life. The settlers were equally self-reliant and trying to build new lives, homes, and civilization as they saw it.

It was a different world. The phases of the moon aren't a focus in modern life. Folks were very aware of the next full moon on the Texas Frontier. The settlers were rugged people and not easily intimidated. Yet they knew Comanches, some of the deadliest warriors in history, preferred raiding by moonlight. Comanches, desperate to fight off an invasion, could be coming for your family at any time. There was no mercy from either side. It could be just as rough when a cavalry unit hit a Native American village.

America is the most prosperous free society in history. This was not built in a day. There were triumphs, tragedies, and injustices along the way. Human nature doesn't change; perhaps that's why we can still relate to stories, thoughts, and experiences of people back in the day.

Finally, for the Ballad of Shannon Dumas series, in efforts to keep speech patterns authentic, Southern accents are written with many words having the last g in a word silent, for example (running) becomes (runnin').

I hope you enjoy this story.

Chapter One
Apple Pie

"Coyote is always out there waiting, and Coyote is always hungry."
— **Navajo Proverb**

Texas 1867

THE AMBUSH WOULD HAVE done the Apaches proud.

She hit us by dawn's early light. A slight aroma of cinnamon wafted through the mornin' mist. It preceded her through the door providin' scant warnin'. Otherwise only the creak of the porch floorboards betrayed her presence. She was carryin' an aromatic iron skillet.

"Good morning, gentlemen."

We both stood as she entered the office. "Good mornin', ma'am."

"I'm looking for Mr. Shannon Dumas."

Rob, my best friend and scrupulous business partner, read the tea leaves instantly and sold me out with a Cheshire cat grin, and an indicative finger.

"I'm Shannon Dumas, ma'am. We aren't quite open yet this mornin', but how can we be of service?"

She gave a matriarchal harumph, instantly assessin' me like an old auctioneer at the cattle markets. By way of emphasis she slammed the ancient cast-iron skillet with a pipin' hot cinnamon apple pie on my desk.

"Mr. Dumas, I'm Mrs. Wilma Eklund."

"Pete's mother?" I smiled. "It's a pleasure to meet..."

She cut me off with decades of matronly umbrage.

"Yes, I am. I'm also president of the Christian Ladies' Aid Society of Dallas. We're affiliated with the church and do bushels of charity work, Christmas baskets and such things, you know. All the best ladies in town are members, and we don't just take in everybody either."

"Yes ma'am. If the society needs a surveyin' project done. Mr. Kantor is actually our senior partner, and..."

"Are you sure you're Shannon Dumas and not his younger brother?"

"Ma'am?"

She eyed the pie for an instant. "From Peter's description I thought you'd be taller, and you're too skinny to be a ranger."

"Ma'am, I'm not a full-time ranger, I just volunteer when they need me."

"I see."

"Ma'am, what exactly is…"

"I have a bone to pick with you, Mr. Shannon Dumas."

I looked over to Rob for help. He was bitin' his tongue to keep a straight face as he abandoned me to collect coffee, forks, and plates.

"Ma'am, if I've given offense somehow, I…"

"Peter told us how you saved his life at that river fight. Yet you have not once accepted my invitation to supper, and we have yet to see you at the monthly square dance. Why is this, young man?"

"Mrs. Eklund, a lot of folks pitched in at the river and as a surveyor, I'm out of Dallas on jobs a good chunk, and…"

"My boy doesn't lie. Peter says a savage was set to club him, and you shot the brute off his horse… The monthly dance is tonight at the Dallas House at six p.m. I'm spending the whole afternoon helping with the decorations and you will be there. I won't take no for an answer."

Her attitude didn't change, but a faint sliver of mischievous sparkle softened the crow's feet at her eyes.

Your best chance to survive an ambush is to charge into it.

"No disrespect, ma'am. I have two left feet, and am engaged to be married, so I don't attend dances and such."

"Does your fiancée forbid it?"

"No, no, nothin' like that."

"It's just one dance. I expect you there at six p.m. sharp. Bring back the pie plate, cleaned proper, when you get a chance."

She smiled for the first time, gave me a motherly pat on the shoulder.

"I leave you gents to the best pie in Texas, baked by my Ingrid."

Then Mrs. Wilma Eklund, president of the Dallas Christian Ladies Aid Society, twirled to the door and marched out of the office without another word or a single look back.

Rob watched the door slam shut and was laughin' so hard he fell to the floor with tears in his eyes.

"Thanks for all your help, by the way…I'm not sharin' a crumb of this apple pie with you for that."

He called my bluff, poured us coffee, and began slicin' the pie.

"Lordy, look at that! Apple pie for breakfast! Shannon my boy, it seems you are in play."

"What? Well, I see where Pete gets his grit." I grinned.

"If I wasn't a happily married man, I'd be tickled pink young Miss Ingrid Eklund has her eye on me."

"Pete's sister? C'mon Rob, everyone knows I'm engaged."

"Shane, I forget how young you are sometimes. Mrs. Eklund, her mama, knows full well René lives out of town."

"How's that?"

"All's fair in love and war."

ᴗᴗᴗᴗᴗᴗᴗ

Dances aren't so bad, actually. My plan was to leave the dance after an hour. I was clean shaven and in my best Sunday shirt by late afternoon. Mrs. Eklund was all smiles at the door and whisked me inside. A chorus of familiar faces chimed in greetin'.

"Good evening, Shane!"

"*El Fusil Largo* can square dance?"

"Of course, he's from New Orleans!"

A good number of my boys were there. Most were rangers like Alligator, Snake, and of course Pete Eklund. The place was decked out nice and all the girls were a sight to behold in their colorful dresses.

Rob Kantor and his wonderful wife, Miss Andrea, were slow dancin' in the corner. I didn't want to interrupt these lovebirds but waved and they nodded, smilin'.

They remind me of my Skipper and Miss Vivian dancin' that day in New Orleans.

Pete was wearin' a fancy new Stetson and brought me a punch while shakin' his head.

"I had no idea my mama was buffaloing you over. I hope you ain't sore?"

"It's all good, she's sweet."

"I swear I told her about René. I truly did."

"I got apple pie for breakfast, I'll dance a few jigs, have a drink with the boys and head out."

We toasted.

"That's a proper new hat, Pete." Then I asked, "I take it Miss Carmen is comin'?"

"I didn't ask her. Chicken, I guess."

"That dog won't hunt."

"Well, Shane, her being Mexican and all. I didn't want her to be uncomfortable if she was the only one here."

"I don't know Pete; pretty girls belong at dances."

The music interrupted us, and Mrs. Eklund wasn't leavin' much to fate. She asked me to help her move the punch bowl to another table. Ingrid Eklund was sitting by that table watchin' all of it in shock.

Her mother began pourin' glasses of punch and said casually, "Thanks Shane, I can handle it from here, why don't you two go dance."

Ingrid stood up glarin' daggers at her mother. She was wearin' a light blue dress, with her hair up, and had the clearest blue eyes I'd ever seen. Her smile was pretty, and she had a lovely voice, but I only had eyes for my René.

"Shane, could we talk a bit. Do you mind?"

"Sure."

Ingrid led me outside to the porch and settled gracefully on the bench. She was fumin' red and near shakin'.

"Shane, I'm so sorry my ma bushwacked you like she did. It's so embarrassing. I...I respect your fiancée. Ma, well Ma.... Is just a force of nature...She gets a notion in her head and heaven help anyone in her way.... I'm an old maid in her eyes at twenty-two.... It's no excuse...please don't be sore."

"Hey, hey now, everythin's fine. She didn't force me to come...It's all good." I looked across the magnificent Texas sunset on the horizon. "I got Swedish cinnamon apple pie for breakfast; all my boys are here. As an engaged man, I can safely say only a fool would balk at sittin' out here with you at sunset."

This calmed her down some.

Then it got dark.

Literally.

Not our conversation, but the sky, as a dark cloud smothered the settin' sun and the winds swirled up.

"May I ask you something?"

"Shoot."

"You will really answer?"

"Yes."

"How did you know with René? I just want to know what that feeling is like."

My answer was cut off by thunder from the clouds and spurs clinkin' heavily on the porch.

The cloud passed to reveal Captain Dalton steppin' out of the desert sunlight.

He tipped his hat to Ingrid, agitated but polite. "Good evening Miss Eklund, Shannon, apologies for the intrusion."

I knew the look in his eyes.

"Hostiles?" I asked. "What about the treaty?"

"I don't think this was Ten Bear's Yamparika. Either way, hostiles hit a stagecoach, just off the Trinity, at Denton a few hours back."

"Captives?"

"One woman of age."

This is bad. We got to hurry.

"How many raiders?"

"A few dozen I reckon."

"I can be ready in ten minutes."

"We could use you on this one. Are the boys inside?"

I nodded and stood to go.

He added, "We'll swing by your office on the way out."

He went in and Ingrid and I shared a moment of silence before we could hear the gasps eminatin' from inside.

"Excuse me, Ingrid."

Rob ran out agitated and put his arm on my shoulder. "Be careful, brother."

We shook.

Ingrid nodded and added, "Come back safe, Shane."

She gave me a peck on the cheek just before I ran for my gear.

ᴜᴜᴜᴜᴜᴜᴜᴜ

The long summer sun was still up when we found the stagecoach. It lay overturned with shattered glass and the contents of broken suitcases spread swirlin' across the prairie.

It was a vulture's feast.

Six dead.

The driver and five male passengers.

Shot and stabbed to pieces.

All scalped and disemboweled with their manhood severed and left in their mouths.

Their soulless eyes stared at us like ghouls as the fleetin' crimson daylight hemorrhaged into cold darkness. I was closin' the last set of eyes when the captain huddled us up.

"The arrows are Comanche, but that spear over there is Kiowa. The manifest reads six passengers including Mr. and Mrs. Gerald Murdock from St. Louis. Boys, I think they took her…"

"How many?"

"Billy reckons at least twenty, and the tracks lead north for the Red River."

"Good eating for Billy," Peter quipped to lighten the mood.

"If they cross the river, we'll never get her back."

Billy Blue was our Tonkawa scout. It takes an Indian to track an Indian and the Tonkawa were sworn enemies of the Comanche. Billy was never wrong about such things, though truth be told he revolted me. Anytime he got the chance he'd slice open a Comanche and eat his liver. Billy believed it gave him the man's strength.

Captain Dalton continued, "Y'all know the drill. We stay on them hard. They don't have much of a lead and might get careless. Cold camps, be ready to rumble, and if they split so do we. I'll lead one section with Billy. Snake, you take the others and Shane if needed. Let's sort this out."

We pushed hard into the rocky desert as coyotes cried out to the moon. The nocturnal breeze wasn't nearly as chillin' as the cold calculus we knew all too well.

Some folks find it incredulous that groups of eight to ten Texas Rangers would tear off into the night after dozens or in some cases hundreds of Comanche raiders.

That's just the way it was.

There were never enough of us, and we knew we must make them pay in blood for each raid, or it would get worse.

The Comanche hated us but didn't like fightin' us. Unlike the army, we traveled light, knew their ways, and all their tricks. They'd separate and slip away whenever possible and only engage us if they had overwhelmin' numbers or we slipped up.

There was little chance of the latter. Captain Dalton was as close to a tactical genius as I ever saw. His instincts and our firepower evened the odds. He always made the right call. We'd have followed him into Hell.

I whispered a prayer for Mrs. Murdock to be brave.

We're comin'.

There wasn't a shred of mercy from either side in Comancheria. The hostiles would scalp, torture and kill near any soul that fell in their hands. All the womenfolk would be violated en masse.

The Comanche might spare children between four and eight to raise as their own. They generally butchered babies since their cryin' could be heard by pursuers. Captive women of age became a grim game of cat and mouse. If they survived the attack they might be violated on the spot. Some were taken captive for the warriors' pleasure.

Generally, they knew we'd come for them like bats out of hell. We knew that if the raiders felt they had enough of a lead they'd stop to take turns with captive women until the novelty wore off. They'd generally murder them after a few days or if we hit them.

However, sometimes we were lucky enough to surprise them while these women were still alive, and we could recover them.

Sometimes.

Regardless, if there were female captives we pushed as hard as possible to catch them those first few days.

ՍՍՍՍՍՍՍՍ

Dawn's gray mist only darkened the situation. The tracks led to a small plum patch swayin' defiantly in the prairie winds.

There was still dew on the bushes and the succulent fruit was an unexpected luxury after a night of water and jerky.

Then we noticed there were already fresh plum skins on the ground. It was clear the Comanche were as fond of plums as we were and had just been here. This definitely got our attention.

It went bad.

Billy Blue found what had once been Mrs. Gerald Murdock just beyond the plum bushes.

I prayed she was in heaven because she'd been cast to hell.

Her pale white skin and big green eyes stuck out from the ochre caliche as if protestin' her fate. More purple plum skins and an empty whiskey bottle lay around her. They'd scalped Mrs. Murdock and cut off her nose, tongue and nipples. Her body was covered in small burns and cuts. There were arrows in her breasts, and they left her violated with a large, gnarled branch in her. Her torn, bloodstained calico dress was tied to an adjacent thorn bush like a fiendish flag flutterin' in the wind.

"They're real close, boys," Captain Dalton said while kneeling over her and closin' her eyes. He kicked the bottle, shatterin' it against the rocks.

"Mount up."

There was no time to bury her.

We wanted their blood.

All of it.

Alligator pointed to movement on the horizon. A large ravine lay due south of us. Two gallopin' riders were churnin' up dust about four hundred yards southwest of the plum patch.

"Hostiles," Pete said. "Runnin' west."

Captain Dalton took this all in and led us after them. I noticed we weren't chasin' them directly but cuttin' right between them and the big ravine.

Once close, the captain wheeled his horse away from the riders and turned back east toward the ravine. We were confused but followed suit.

"Ignore them boys, form the wedge. Wedge up.... Wedge.... Here they come!"

We would wedge up or gallop with our horses as close as possible in a charge. We were always outnumbered, and this arrowhead-like formation concentrated our firepower and left no gaps for the enemy to ride through.

We still didn't see a thing at the ravine but bolted for it anyway.

We trusted our captain.

He was always right.

A few dozen Comanche warriors suddenly rode up out of the ravine whoopin' their war cries framed by the sun. They charged back into us.

If Captain Dalton hadn't seen through the ruse, they'd have hit us from the rear with the risin' sun blindin' us.

The sun was still in our eyes, but instead we were ready for them. We spurred our mounts into them, waitin' for the command to fire. They came in shriekin', a blood-chillin' wave in war paint, churnin' up the dusty red earth between us.

Arrows and bullets whizzed past us.

I had a Comanche lined up in my sights when a screamin' crimson spray splattered me across the face. The ranger to my left had caught an arrow through the eye.

"BUST THEM!"

We fired on the captain's signal, at a range of about fifty yards, with blindin' closin' speed.

My first shot hit a black and red painted Comanche in the chest, blowin' him off his horse.

An arrow swished past my face from the right.

Another snapped into my saddle, just missin' my leg.

Just before both sides crashed, amidst swirlin' smoke, screams, and bloodthirsty rage, a wall of concentrated lead decimated the center of their battle line. The four to five Comanches in the middle were simply blown off their painted war ponies like leaves in a storm. We rode right through this bloody gap as trained.

Hostiles couldn't match the force of our repeatin' guns up close. We needed this advantage. No one fights as well as a Comanche on horseback.

No one.

Off to the side I saw a Comanche leap nimbly off his horse and knife a fallen ranger who was tryin' to stand. He'd pulled back the man's head, scalped him and raised his bloody arms to the heavens roarin' in triumph.

I kicked him at full force from my streakin' horse. The boot's impact knocked him sprawlin' in a cloud of dust. My first round caught him in the stomach, and I fired again into his chest.

Movement to the left caught my eye.

I whirled but knew it was too late.

A massive grinnin' brave was right on top of me with a wicked smile.

His leveled war lance was set to skewer me.

Oh god.

The brave's black and white painted face suddenly exploded like a blood-filled balloon as my horse screamed. He'd taken that lance intended for me.

My dear horse dropped to his knees and fell to his side with a dusty thud.

I jumped off just in time.

I scrambled to a knee, dirt stingin' my eyes, and pulled the Henry from the saddle scabbard.

Why am I alive?

What saved me?

A gore-splattered Captain Dalton, with his smokin' shotgun, winked at me from just further left.

I nodded thanks.

My Colt tracked another mounted brave hurtlin' past me to the right.

He somehow disappeared just as I fired.

A whizzin' bullet simultaneously blew off my hat.

This magnificent warrior had ducked off the side of his war pony like they were one single creature. My shot flew harmlessly through the spot he'd just been. He'd returned fire, at a full gallop, hangin' from under his horse's neck.

An inch lower would have taken my head with it.

My poor horse's screams shattered through my ears. I shot him in the head and slipped in the expandin' pool of his blood.

A fallen ranger's mount was ten yards away.

I sprinted over coughin' dust and jumped on in a confusin' cloud of smoke and screams.

The Comanche battle line was split in half like a wave crashin' on an immovable boulder. Captain Dalton wheeled his horse around in pursuit before we were even clear of them. Those of us left spun our horses around to reform the wedge.

"After them, boys! STAY ON THEM. STAY ON THEM!" roared the captain. "BUST THEM!"

Another concentrated wall of lead smacked into them. Instead of turnin' back for us the Comanches broke off in panic, even though they outnumbered us.

It wasn't fear so much as surprise.

They outnumbered us and had expected to hit us from the rear as we chased the bait. Instead we charged into them and punched right through their center with superior firepower, then we were behind them chasin' and killin' as fast as we could.

Panic and fear are contagious.

It was like a grizzly bear decidin' a ferocious wolverine wasn't worth it. Once a few of them broke the rest followed suit. In a battle this is when the real killin' starts, when one side is tryin' to escape. Captain Dalton blew off the back of a fleein' brave's head with his scattergun. I shot at least one more off his war pony in pursuit.

The gap widened between us after about a hundred yards of chase. Comanche horses were so much faster than ours. They could outrun or catch us at will.

The captain reared up his horse in a cloud of dust yellin', "HALT UP...CEASE FIRE...STOP, BOYS." He'd taken an arrow to the shoulder and was noddin' to us.

"We bloodied them good, boys.... Top notch.... Top notch."

"You're hit, sir!"

"I'll live...Alligator, keep watch they don't come back. The rest of you see to our wounded and kill theirs."

The lord may have mercy, but there's none in Comancheria.

I hadn't scalped anyone at that point, but I'd be lyin' if I said some of us didn't return the favor before shootin' every fallen Comanche again in the head. I retrieved my hat and was more focused on our wounded.

A chill went through me as I recognized a ranger on the ground. He'd taken an eight-foot Kiowa lance through the guts and was sprawled on his side. He was starin' into the horizon as I took him in my lap.

"Pete, it's Shane."

"Shane...It hurts.... It hurts...I'm thirsty."

I gave him some water as he smiled through blood-stained teeth.

"I don't want to die, Shane.... I..."

"Relax, we'll get you patched up, just relax."

He laughed and said faintly, "No, I'm as broken as your hat...Take mine, Shane. Take my hat, okay?"

"Pete, breathe, stay with me...We'll get you to the doc in Dallas."

His bloody broken hand touched his hat. "Take it, okay?"

I nodded and put his bloodstained Stetson on my head

"I'll have to buy you a fancy new one."

He smiled again.

"I'm cold...it's so cold." He shook his head. "Tell my people...I...You know."

I looked him in the eyes. "I promise, Pete."

He was shiverin'. I held him close and warm as possible, as the light faded out of his eyes.

Chapter Two
Harper's Weekly

"What the people believe is true."
— **Dakota Proverb**

Two weeks later

Captain Dalton walked into my office with a dark smile on a sunny day.

"How's the shoulder, sir?"

"Doc Parrish and a week's rest can work wonders on a man."

"Good to hear. Did you keep the arrowhead as a souvenir?"

"I'd have quite a collection if I did." He laughed. "Can I buy you a steak, Shane?"

"Sir, every time you offer steak, and especially use my first name, bad things are afoot...Hostiles?"

He laughed. "This might be even worse."

"Do I need my horse and guns?"

"No, no." He shook his head. "Well, maybe."

"Sir?"

"Let's eat, I'll explain."

At the Yellow Rose, he barely touched his steak but took down his whiskey. He was polite enough to let me finish my plate before gettin' down to business.

"I got to testify against that corrupt Indian agent at Fort Worth, I'll be gone a day or so."

"You need me to help Marshal Irvin if need be while you're out?"

"No, Alligator and Snake can handle that."

"Okay?"

"There's a hack reporter in town from back east. *Harper's Weekly*, I think. He wants to do a story on the rangers. The mayor ordered we cooperate. Good publicity for Dallas and such."

"I see."

"I honestly think Alligator or Snake would shoot him within minutes of meeting him. I'm not sure I'd press charges, to be honest."

I laughed. "He's that bad?"

"He's one of them utterly clueless, know-it-all, East Coast liberals dumb enough to fall into a barrel of tits and come out sucking their thumbs."

"Why me, sir?" I laughed. "I'm not even a full-time ranger?"

"Because our already poor funding could be at risk if it gets political." He shook his head. "Shane, I know I'd toss him out a window in five minutes. You're patient, educated back east as well, and you only kill when necessary, so far."

"What's his deal?"

"I'm not sure, but will you handle this for us?"

"You just want me to answer his questions?"

"Yup. Have a coffee, tell the truth, and try not to shoot him."

"I can handle that, sir."

ႱႱႱႱႱႱႱႱ

The knock came on the office door just as the coffee pot ran dry. A corpulent, pasty-skinned man sauntered into the office. He was dressed like a riverboat gambler and fannin' sweat away from his beet-red face.

"Mister Dumas? I'm Reed Sanders from *Harper's Weekly*."

I shook his pink clammy hand.

"I'm Shannon Dumas. It's hot, sir. Take off your jacket. Can I offer you some water or coffee?"

"Water, please. I don't drink coffee. Do you have mint tea by chance?"

"I'm sorry sir, we only have coffee, and the pot's dry. Have some of this water."

He gulped down the glass I'd filled and wiped his face dry with a handkerchief.

I poured him another glass.

"I came all the way from Washington. I must say, Washington is looking better to me all the time...I understand you are from back east as well?"

"Yes, sir. New Orleans."

"Why would anyone leave civilization for Texas?"

"The war wrecked a lot of plans, sir."

"You were too young for the war. In fact you're too young to be a ranger, or a surveyor, aren't you?"

"I didn't serve if that's what you're askin', but I volunteer with the rangers as needed. Mr. Kantor took me in a few years back and recently made me a partner."

"Why do they call you *Fusil Largo?*"

"It's not important."

"So they pawn me off on a wet behind the ears, part-time ranger, to spin up an endearing story?"

I looked him directly in the eyes.

"Is that what you think of me, Mr. Sanders?"

"No offense, young man."

Strike one.

"How can I help?"

"I'm after a story on the Wells Fargo stage holdup, in April, by the Red River."

"They heard of that back in the Capital?"

"Your bungled investigations with three dead stage passengers get a lot of publicity."

"Why the trip to Dallas if you already know the story so well?"

"Our readers need the real story, not some romanticized account."

Strike two.

"Romanticized?" I smirked. "Sir, things are a bit more Hobbesian on the frontier."

"You can't know Hobbes?"

"I looked at the pictures in a big leather book once."

"Sarcasm doesn't suit you, young man. Summarize Hobbes if you've actually read him."

"Life is nasty, brutish, and short, which is what this interview will be if you insult me again."

"I see."

"I actually don't think you do. The South is old-fashioned, but Texas is Texas. The code here is men are born and raised not to take an insult. If you insult a man here you best back it up. Now I'm not a native Texan either but I respect local traditions. I'd just ask you to leave, but with most folks down here, be polite or there will be blood."

"How draconian. Let me guess, next you'll tell me the Comanche took scalps before white folk showed them how?"

Strike three. You're out.

"I don't know sir, Mesopotamia is likely the cradle of civilization, and Hammurabi's Code wasn't so different."

"Your education is noted, young man."

"Sir, if you value the truth, may I be honest with you?"

"Always."

"I'll give you the benefit of the doubt since you've been ignorantly condescending on multiple levels. You come across as a pompous, know-it-all windbag, with a sophomoric agenda and a story written before he left Maryland. You wouldn't last a lick on the frontier. You fancy yourself some sort of crusadin' intellectual, the reality is I doubt you could hit water if you fell out of a boat. You need to sell your readers spice for their boring, comfortable lives. So, you will paint us as impossibly noble heroes like that ridiculous fluff piece on that jackass Custer, or crucify us as incompetent, barbaric frontier brutes."

He smiled for the first time. "You could be an editor."

"I'd rather be captured by the Comanche."

"Understood. Did you investigate the hold-up?"

"No, sir. Captain Dalton was there. He'd have the facts. Maybe just talk with him?"

"Facts dripping with swagger, no doubt. Perhaps you can tell me what you know about it. It's about time somebody wrote a story on the frontier the way it really is and not the way it's pictured in exaggerated accounts."

"You're the gent to write that story, huh?"

"I'm a hard man to fool, Mr. Dumas. I've been trained by experts."

"Experts who've learnt from books or universities, or experts who've actually been in the arena?"

"Who's being condescending now, Ranger?"

"You expect nothin' but tall tales?"

"It appears habitual out West. A story isn't a story if it isn't three times life size. Everything's bigger in Texas, right?"

"Mr. Sanders, you won't get a tall tale from me. In fact, you won't get any story at all."

"The Texas Rangers must account for how they bungled things and let the crooks escape."

"You figure that's the way it was?"

"It's well known one of them was badly wounded and couldn't travel far. There are scouts in the West who can track a desperado's trail."

"Have you ever tracked anyone in the desert? Have you ever hunted or even held a gun in your hand?"

"That doesn't matter. I know there are experts here with those skills."

"Please produce that scout then. Two days had passed by the time someone discovered that stage. I wasn't there, but that trail was a full three days old, and wind swept before the rangers got there. The bandits could have veered off a hundred miles in any direction. We have roughly three dozen rangers coverin' a wild, dangerous territory larger than some US states. Then there's the

Comanches, well they are one serious bunch if you get my drift. Which is why folks like me volunteer."

"So you've given up. Too few rangers and too much land is your excuse. You're letting the killer bandits get away."

"Excuse? They likely won't get away. Someone will see them or say somethin', or they will slip up."

"You're going to catch them from here in your office, Ranger Dumas? Is this how the taxpayers' money is spent in Texas?"

"You're writing your story before it's finished, Mr. Sanders? In that case please excuse me, sir. I've taken time out of my workday to indulge you, but I've had my fill. If your story flops, maybe add a few chapters, throw in a white whale, and call it the great American novel?...Oh wait, that's been done."

"I like you, young man. Good day." He laughed, put on his coat and left.

Rob had heard the entire conversation and watched him walk away.

"Shane, you rarely show this eloquent side of you. It's hilarious. Sometimes I think you could sit on a tub of ice cream and tell the flavor. If the Comanche don't cut your balls off I bet you'll end up an attorney."

"That'll be the day."

ʊʊʊʊʊʊʊ

Mr. Sanders stuck around Dallas for another week annoyin' every creature under the merciless Texas sun. He must have been tight with the holy ghost since somehow no one cut him or stomped him into a bloody pulp. If so, that wasn't the only supernatural rumor floatin' around the Dallas saloons.

Not a week after my ordeal by interview, I saw Alligator and the captain saddlin' up their mounts near sunset.

"What gives?"

"Ghosts." Alligator grinned.

"Huh?"

"You know that wanderin' snake oil salesman Mr. Trudeau?"

"I guess so."

"He was caught in the rains last night and tried to bed down in that old, deserted Collins cabin to the north."

"The one folks say is haunted," Alligator added.

"Well, if it was spirits they shoot rifles," Captain Dalton explained. "There were at least two riflemen according to Mr. Trudeau. He took off running and didn't stop until he got to Dallas."

"Why would anyone stay out there so exposed in Comancheria?" I thought out loud. "Unless they're hidin' from somethin'?"

The captain nodded. "Could we borrow your Sharps?"

"I can do better than that, sir. Give me few minutes."

We rode north by silent moonlight. A few hours after the moon popped, I had a familiar naggin' feelin' botherin' me. I could tell Alligator and the captain felt it as well.

"We're being followed, sir," Alligator said.

The captain nodded and we cleared off the trail with guns ready.

The man followin' us was alone, made us much noise as a circus, and could barely ride a horse.

The captain sighed. "What are you doin' out here, Mr. Sanders? I almost had Alligator knife you, with all that racket, we'd already be scalped if there were any hostiles within ten miles."

"That's one way to squash a story. I heard you might be after the holdup bandits. I've been tracking you rangers."

"Tracking?" Alligator chortled. "We're riding on the main road."

"Mr. Sanders, this isn't a church picnic. If it is them, it could be half a dozen, and they've already killed in cold blood."

"I want to be in on the scoop. I want to watch the legendary Texas Rangers earn their pay and catch the desperadoes."

"You need to head back for Dallas."

"I will not. Freedom of the press!"

"Can I just stomp him now, sir?" Alligator asked. "It would be more merciful."

The captain sighed. "I'm tempted, but it's too dark and Mr. Sanders here likely ends up scalped or giving some poor bear indigestion. I don't think he can even follow a trail back to Dallas, and we'll have to waste even more time looking for him."

"Now you're being sensible, Captain."

The captain's tone hardened. "All right, Mr. Sanders, you can come, but you will keep your mouth shut and do as told."

"Understood."

"I hope so, sir," the captain said while brandishin' his Bowie. "Because if you foul up and put my men in danger, I will gut you and leave you out for the coyotes...Are we clear?"

Mr. Sander's eyes got as wide as saucers takin' in that steel blade by moonlight.

He nodded.

∪∪∪∪∪∪∪∪

The old Collins cabin was in a large circular meadow ringed by a thick tree line. The remnants of a charred, dilapidated barn lay next to it. A densely wooded hill was about a hundred yards to the south. The original owners had cleared back the brush on all sides to hinder raidin' Indians from sneakin' up close.

Dawn found us at the edge of the tree line as the captain took it all in.

"Boys, anyone in there has decent fields of fire in every direction. Mr. Dumas, from a good tree up that hill you can cover the whole area with your Sharps. Bust anything that even blinks wrong. Alligator and I will get as close as possible using the barn as cover. Mr. Sanders, you will stay here. Be silent, stay under cover, and watch the horses."

"I can't see anything for my story laying low."

"There won't be a story if they blow your head off…Or if you put my men in danger."

"Why go on foot. You could be right up on the cabin in seconds with the horses. I've read Western peace officers never dismount if possible."

"Sir, can I just gag and tie up this fool now before he gets someone hurt?" Alligator glared.

"I want to do the story right."

The captain hissed, "Keep your voice down. We're too close to earshot."

Mr. Sanders nodded as I left for the hill. I was in position before long and signaled the captain from up a tree.

Alligator and the captain crawled out into the meadow tryin' to use an old, petrified log for cover.

Then all hell broke loose.

They'd been seen.

Rifle fire from the cabin began pepperin' their fallen log with lead.

I counted three rifles firin' furiously from the cabin.

The captain and Alligator were pinned down.

"WE'RE TEXAS RANGERS. HOLD YOUR FIRE!"

Whoever was in the cabin kept firin' from different windows.

I began blastin' each window out with the Sharps.

A scream from the cabin told me I'd hit one.

Alligator and the captain began returning fire as rounds ricocheted all around them.

Suddenly a figure burst out of the cabin screamin' as bullets zinged in every direction. He was tryin' to zigzag and yellin', "DON'T SHOOT! PLEASE!"

Bullets were hittin' at his feet, and he went down hard screamin' about twenty yards in front of the Alligator and the captain.

It looked like a teenage boy.

He was cryin' and crawlin' for the log.

Alligator sprinted into heavy fire to retrieve him while the captain and I covered him as best we could. He scooped the boy up and somehow made it back to the tree line.

There were only two rifles firin' from the cabin now.

I watched Alligator crawl back to the log.

Then it got quiet.

Captain Dalton signaled to me he thought there were only two bandits left in the cabin.

I signaled back yes. He made the hand signal for fire.

Exactly—if it's just bandits in there, let's burn them out.

The captain crawled back into the tree line, then back.

He nodded. Alligator and I began blanketin' the cabin with coverin' fire while the captain sprinted for the barn. It was close, bullets were kicking at his heels, but he made it.

It got quiet again.

The captain roared, "TEXAS RANGERS...COME OUT WITH YOUR HANDS UP!"

"GO TO HELL!"

They began shootin' at the barn, as Alligator and I fired into the cabin.

"WE'LL BURN YOU OUT!"

The captain began shootin' burnin' arrows at the cabin. The third or fourth one caught in the roof, and it began smokin'.

The cabin was still shootin' like crazy as the blaze began to catch in earnest.

I knew what came next.

A bandit with a shotgun suddenly sprang out the back door of the cabin to escape.

I put him down with the Sharps in a dusty thud.

The last one in the smokin' cabin saw there was no escape.

A voice yelled from the cabin.

"OKAY, I'M COMIN' OUT! DON'T SHOOT!"

"HANDS UP! MOVE SLOW!" the captain hollered.

A big man in a black hat came out of the cabin slowly with his hands up. The captain had him lie down and cuffed him as the cabin roof collapsed in flames.

When I got to the tree line, Mr. Sanders was sittin' up against a tree with blood all over him, and the boy in his arms.

"You hit?"

"Huh? No, no, it's the boy's blood.... His name was Timmy Jenkins."

I nodded.

The reporter's voice cracked. "He was cryin' for his mama.... Who was this boy? Why did they take him. Why shoot him?"

"I don't know."

Papers from saddlebags in the barn confirmed these were the bandits who hit that stage. We secured the prisoner and buried the boy and the bandit who'd made a run for it. Mr. Sanders was quiet and pitched in hard with his shovel.

On the ride back to Dallas, the captain and Alligator flanked the cuffed prisoner while Mr. Sanders and I followed.

He stopped his horse and looked back at the cabin's smoky embers.

"Is it always like this?"

"Sometimes worse."

"I got my story, I guess."

"I could care less about your story."

"I didn't mean it like that...I...I've never dug a grave before."

"It gives a man perspective. You don't need to dig more than one though."

"Mr. Dumas, do you want to hear my ideas on the West?"

I was good and sour.

"Not particularly. It's a free country though. I'm sure you will get big headlines desribin' how inept the rangers are. We let the bandits roam wild for months and got a young boy killed, right? Then a wet behind the ears part-time ranger guns down a bandit runnin' away?.... I should have just shot him in the leg, right? It's so easy to do that, right? Of course, everyone knows it would have turned out better if we'd just charged up there on horses like the experts say…No romanticized Texas tall tales here, right?"

"They would have blasted down the horses once they heard them, and any bandit brazen enough to shoot a hostage boy could kill anyone else he encountered."

"You learn fast, Mr. Sanders."

His voice faltered. "I'm writing that the frontier is a beautiful, savage place working toward civilization. The rangers are trying to keep the peace as best they can. Sometimes they are heroic, like Alligator risking a hail of bullets to save the boy; sometimes bad things happen. I'm going to say all of it, the good, the bad, the ugly, warts and all is how progress is defined. I'll tell them I believe someday Texas will be as civilized and safe as New York City."

"I don't know about all that. There's monsters in this world, you got to face them down."

"You're a philosopher, young man. Imagine an educated, sharp-shooting, gentleman ranger. You will fascinate my readers."

"Mr. Sanders, would you do me a favor?"

"Of course."

"No disrespect, but kindly leave me out of your story."

"Mr. Dumas, I saw it firsthand. You gunned down two bandits at range and covered your comrades."

"We don't keep track of such things."

"You have my word."

"Appreciated."

"My editor will likely reject what I'll write now anyway."

"Alligator's name is Allen Johnson, by the way."

"I'll make sure to spell it right."

"Aren't there rough parts of New York as well?"

"Yes."

"Mr. Sanders, you've gotten a taste of reality now. Folks wonder why we don't talk about days like this. I don't care to share it with strangers, and why would you burden friends and family with what a cryin' gutshot boy dyin' in your arms feels like?"

He nodded.

"I don't know what to say." His eyes were moist. "I understand if the answer is no, but when we get back to Dallas can I buy you gentlemen a drink?"

I looked him in the eyes and saw he meant it.

"I could use a drink."

CHAPTER THREE
RAID

"We will be known forever by the tracks we leave."
— Blackfoot Proverb

Two months later

VULTURES CIRCLED LAZILY IN the blood-red sky. They languished as if they had all the time in the world or knew somethin' we didn't. We didn't need the dawn birds to guide us. Hazy plumes of greasy smoke guided us across the dusky Texas plain like a lighthouse in a storm.

We'd seen it before but each time I'd pray to never see it again. The gustin' winds were kind that mornin'. So far, you couldn't smell it. That sickly sweet smell all too common to

Comancheria. A smell you never forget, one that lingers in your soul long after dusty clothes are scrubbed clean.

Captain Dalton halted us.

"Eyes peeled, boys, fire only on my signal, let's sort this out."

He wasn't takin' any chances. Part of this was well-honed frontier instincts. Also, there were only three of us, instead of a full contingent of Texas Rangers. I'd volunteered and been deputized at least a dozen times. We'd shared some rough scrapes together.

It got to the point where the captain issued me a badge and said only wear it when we need you. Given the life expectancy of rangers in Comancheria, there were no shortages of badges or volunteer opportunities.

That was the case this mornin' when I saw Captain Dalton and Alligator ridin' past my office. Both were sportin' grim looks. The captain mentioned there was a raid last night just outside of town. When I replied that was close enough for the soldiers from Fort Worth to handle, he agreed and took a deep breath.

"They hit the Eklund place."

That changed everythin'.

My heart sank as I rushed for my guns and horse.

Pete Eklund had bled out in my arms just shy of twenty. He'd been in a dozen bloody battles, but confessed he'd never once kissed a girl. I doubt he'd even had time to ever hold a girl's hand.

He'd had eyes for a young señorita named Carmen. I'd been the one to close his eyes.

Alligator, a powerfully built man, whose moniker came from an infamous wrestlin' match with an unfortunate reptile, was shakin' his head in disbelief. We hadn't had an Indian raid in months and none this close to Dallas.

Now this.

Most likely Comanches or Kiowa that hit the Eklund place, maybe Apaches. The Comanches and their Kiowa allies were supremely confident horsemen and preferred fluid open plains battle. The Apaches liked to strike from ambush.

For some reason my thoughts stretched back to my grandpa, Skipper, explainin' the difference between African lions and leopards. A lion is supremely confident and powerful, much deadlier if he reaches you, but he proclaims his presence with bone-chillin' roars. Not so the leopard, who won't make a sound until you pass, then tears out the back of your neck. The Comanches fought like lions and the Apaches struck like leopards. Skipper always thought leopards to be more lethal.

Both are deadly.

We wouldn't be the first pursuin' rangers ambushed after a raid, but not on Captain Dalton's watch. It was too late for the Eklund family other than deprivin' these vultures of their feast. The scatterin' big-winged birds lingered a bit too long. Their cold dark eyes smirked at us like undertakers at fussy folks who don't realize we are all future business.

In a way, all raided homesteads are eerily similar. What had once been the Eklund cabin, corral and barn, were smoldering charred ruins. A body by the corral, another in the doorway, one lyin' just outside the porch and the last one sprawled in the ashes of the barn. All but one scalped and mutilated.

"Just four to the family, Alligator?"

"Yeah."

A gray-haired corpse lay sprawled, in a pool of blood, between the house and barn. It was still holdin' a bloodstained Bowie.

"This must be the father, Captain," Alligator said.

"Yeah, he was coming out of the cabin to help his boy over there by the corral... Well,

he cut one before he died."

"Yeah."

All their longhorns had been slaughtered or run off. Alligator pulled a lance out of a prize jersey cow.

"Kiowa?" I asked.

The captain nodded. "I'd reckon a mix of Kiowa and Comanche by the way they're scalped."

He took a knee by a crumpled body at the corral. It was Pete's younger brother Johan. He'd been scalped and shot at least four times. Blood trails circled his body. This told us he took at least one raider with him. The Indians carry off their dead whenever possible.

"The boy fought hard." The captain sighed.

"He wasn't a day over fourteen," Alligator said, pickin' up the boy's spent shotgun.

We found the remains of Pete's mama in what was left of the barn. She lay sprawled and scalped. Her skirts were raised over her head.

"She brought me apple pie," I said to no one.

"They moved her here," Captain Dalton said softly. He lowered her dress back down over her naked legs.

The next thing I saw made me heave. What was left of Ingrid lay charred in the door of the cabin. She'd been shot a dozen times. A broken rifle and two pistols were at her side. There were three blood trails not far from the porch.

It's hard to see a dead woman. Especially one so young and joyful who flirted with you.

"She's the only one not scalped," I noticed.

"Do you think they..." Alligator asked.

"No" The captain cut him off. "Also, they didn't scalp her out of respect. She must have fought like a harpy from Hell for her mama. The poor girl made her stand at the door."

This was the end of the Eklund clan. Their blood was gone from the Earth now. Everythin' their ancestors had endured across oceans of time ended here. My god, it's a cold world.

Then I realized somethin'. "Captain, it was definitely Kiowa but not a single arrow anywhere, and they took the horses but left the guns?"

Alligator snorted. "Hostiles never raid without bows or leave guns behind."

They didn't bring bows because they had enough guns, and the only reason they left the Eklund's guns behind was if the raiders already had better guns...

Man for man the Comanches could outride, out track and outlast us in the desert. Back in the day, they could get twenty arrows off in the time it took to reload a single shot rifle. Indians were for the most part master archers but average shots with their old single shot rifles.

Repeatin' rifles and revolvers evened the odds for us.

Frankly, if there were more Comanches and they all had repeating rifles, things might have turned out much uglier for Texas.

'There's hell to pay." Captain Dalton's reply was chillin'. "I think they have repeaters, Spencers to be exact."

The Army's lethal Spencer rifles could fire seven shots before reloadin'. It was a hangin' offense to sell repeatin' rifles to the Indians. Of course, greedy traders knew the Indians would pay any price for them.

This was a sobering proposition.

He tossed me a spent Spencer cartridge case from the mud.

"Do you think they scavenged a few or they have a seller?" I asked.

"They have enough that a war party didn't bring bows on a blood raid," he replied.

Alligator whistled in response.

I didn't want to think about facin" Comanches with Spencer rifles.

We heard horses on the horizon.

"Hey, look over yonder, Captain."

"Huh?"

"They're coming over the rise."

"Yeah."

"They're a little late. A whole cavalry troop?"

"So were we."

"Yup."

"Likely from Fort Worth. I wonder who's in command. Can't tell yet."

"They're spreadin' out. Maybe they think we're Indians.... They're fixin' to charge."

"Yeah, they're playing it safe. That's all...Just stand easy."

They rode up facin' us with guns leveled.

An impossibly young lieutenant we hadn't seen before glared at us.

"What are you men doing here?"

Captain Dalton's glance told Alligator and me to keep mum.

"Well, speak up!"

The captain's voice was firm. "We're looking around, Lieutenant. Same as you."

"Don't be insolent, sir," he replied.

A sergeant pointed to the ground behind us.

"What is it, Sergeant?"

"A Spencer rifle lying there, sir."

"You're right, Sergeant. Disarm these men."

"Yes, sir."

Captain Dalton replied, "If I were you, I'd stand back, Sergeant."

The lieutenant snapped, "Don't be fools. There are ten of us and seventy men behind us. You can't fight the whole army."

The sergeant retrieved the Spencer but left us be.

The captain gave the young officer a look you give an irritatin' puppy.

The lieutenant was gettin' hot. "I said disarm them, completely. You make one move for your guns, we blast you."

The captain pondered on it, then dropped his gun belt in silence. We followed suit.

Alligator's glance asked, *When are we going to tell these fools who we are?*

I shook my head.

"Now, will you tell me what you're doing here?"

We didn't bother to reply.

"No. Then you men are prisoners. I'm taking you to Fort Worth. Sergeant, secure these men."

"Yes, sir."

"Then let's bury these pour souls. Shouldn't take more than an hour."

∪∪∪∪∪∪∪

Fort Worth was a dozen dusty miles due west.

"Lieutenant Ellis reporting with the prisoners, Major."

"Bring them in."

We stood at the desk.

"Are these your prisoners, Lieutenant Ellis?"

"Yes, sir."

"I see."

"They were at the scene of the raid with a Spencer rifle, and I thought they might have something to do with the missing guns. They wouldn't talk and they showed signs of resistance, sir."

The major smiled at Captain Dalton.

"Why wouldn't you talk?"

"Curiosity."

"Curious about what?"

"We hadn't heard about any Kiowas being on the war path, for starters."

"Yes, what else?"

"We found that Spencer rifle there and figured someone's been gun running to the tribes. But when the lieutenant came up with his troop, I reckoned that there was more to it."

"Why?"

"Well, he was more interested in us than pursuing that war party…What's going on…Major?"

The lieutenant interjected. "Watch your tone, sir."

The major smiled again. "I'll handle this, Lieutenant."

"Yes, sir."

Major Duvall stood and addressed the captain again.

"You know about the Red River reservation?"

"Well, I heard that you're holding a couple of thousand Kiowas and Comanches."

"Correct. Except for one thing."

"What?"

"We lost a few of them."

"What's a few?"

"Thirty to forty."

"That's a few?"

"You just saw the results."

"Yeah… Who's their leader?"

"A young Kiowa named Red Wolf."

"Why didn't the lieutenant go after him instead of stopping to take us prisoner?"

"His orders were to catch whoever is selling those rifles."

"Fine, but he still might have been able to run down Red Wolf's party."

"Well, what good would that do?"

"How about keep another family from getting massacred like the Eklunds?"

"You know I didn't mean it that way. Even if we caught Red Wolf, he'd be replaced overnight. As long as modern rifles are available, braves on that reservation will hear it and join the renegades."

"Patrol the reservation."

"We don't have enough men for effective patrols."

"If this gun running isn't stopped, this situation will get out of hand.... We'll all be lucky to survive it."

"I know."

"There might be a way I can fix this."

Lieutenant Ellis snapped, "You are still under arrest, sir."

Captain Dalton rolled his eyes.

The major explained, "Lieutenant Ellis, you're new out here. You did right bringing this here motley crew in. They smell of horses and caliche. They are as disreputable looking a bunch as I've seen in ages."

"Yes, sir. That's what I thought. I expect they are troublemakers of some sort."

Alligator cut wind in response.

"My god man, what do you eat." Major Duvall fanned his nose. "Take them out, give them a bath and clean shirts. Bring them back."

"Yes, sir."

"Then have three extra places set for them in the officers' mess."

"The officers' mess, sir?"

"Yes, it's been quite a spell since Captain Dalton and his boys have visited Fort Worth."

The lieutenant's eyes were as wide as saucers. "This is Captain Dalton of the Texas Rangers?"

The major nodded. "Yes, and that big fellow is called Alligator. The other one the Comanche call *Fusil Largo*."

"Fusil Largo?"

"Yes, it's bad Spanish for 'Long Rifle.' Don't they teach languages at West Point anymore?"

"Yes, sir, they do."

"Pray tell, Lieutenant, why do you imagine the Comanche call this ranger *Fusil Largo?*"

"I imagine he shoots well, sir."

"I shoot well." The major added, "Mr. Dumas can put a round through a gnat's ass at a hundred yards...He might be the best shot in Texas...Think about that statement."

Realization set in for Lieutenant Ellis.

Major Duvall smiled. "I would have arrested these scoundrels too, if I didn't know them so well."

Captain Dalton said, "No hard feelings, Lieutenant. You were following orders, albeit foolish ones with flawed intelligence."

Major Duvall narrowed his eyes. "What's that mean, Captain?"

"I'm sorry to interfere, Major. It's not my army anymore."

"Speak up."

"I meant intelligence in the military sense."

"Continue."

"You can scour the prairie looking for gun runners you'll likely never find...But Red Wolf finds them."

"I've asked our Delaware scouts."

"The tribes hate your Indian scouts worse than they hate you."

"I know."

"Is Chief Ten Bears on the Red River reservation?"

"He is. Why?"

"I might have a talk with him. He's sure to know the score."

"Impossible."

"Why?"

"The Comanches are too restless. I wouldn't dare send you and guards into that camp."

"I'll risk it alone."

"They'd kill any white man who walked in there alone."

"I'll try to reach Ten Bears first...He knows me."

"I can't allow it."

"Well, it's a good thing we don't report to the army."

"They will slaughter you, There's over a thousand Comanches in that camp."

"Better that than a full-scale frontier war. We'll know in a few nights. It might help get visions of the Eklund homestead out of my mind before I try to sleep."

Major Duvall finally nodded. "We'll get you a fresh mount."

"Captain, I'm comin' with," I said.

"No, Mr. Dumas. Thank you though."

"It was a statement not a request, sir."

He shook his head.

I removed my badge.

Folks who've never served in harm's way can never understand the brotherhood of warriors.

It's the only beauty in war.

I recall a ranger's funeral where his widow cursed us. She said we just got him killed and didn't really know him. We took it in silence and tried to comfort her.

The truth was, we knew her husband better than her. I knew his most private thoughts. I knew her favorite foods, about their first kiss. I knew how her flapjacks were always a bit dry and that peas made her pass wind. I knew about all their silly arguments and how he hoped to someday talk her into moving to California. I knew his guilt when a grateful farm girl kissed him full on the mouth for rescuin' her family from Apaches.

I knew him.

Every little detail.

I was the one to wipe the tears from his face at the end, and close his eyes afterwards. We don't tell the families hurtful things. It's the warrior's code.

"I'm comin' with or without it."

The Kantors, Father King and the rangers were all the family I had left in the world.

"Mr. Dumas...Er... Shane...The major is right. Given their mood, the Comanche may talk, or they could simply scalp us and cut our balls off."

There's no way in hell I let Captain Dalton face this alone.

I didn't reply.

The number of people in your life who'd kill or die for you has always been my measure of wealth.

"OK, thanks Shane. Put your badge back on. I surely thought you were smarter than this."

Chapter Four
Red River

"Less thunder in the mouth and more lightning in the hand."
– Apache Proverb

The following night

A COYOTE HOWLED INTO a star-crossed Stygian sky.

Captain Dalton cursed under his breath.

"Godammit! Not now!"

"Sir, just a coyote. I wonder if they are as lonely as they sound?"

"Not to the Indians. Coyote is a bad omen."

"I see."

Toss your gun belt across your saddle, Mr. Dumas."

I did as instructed.

"The gun won't do you any good if all these Kiowas decide they want us."

"Yes, sir."

"Keep only that Derringer hidden in your boot. If it goes bad.... Eat it."

We knew better than to be taken alive in Comancheria. We'd seen the tortures they inflicted on prisoners.... Especially their womenfolk, who'd make every man's greatest fear dull-knifed reality.

"How about the Bowie?"

He laughed. "Let's not give their squaws any ideas."

"The camp is sleepin'."

"There're thousands in this camp. They ain't all asleep."

"I can feel eyes on us."

"Think of the bright side, Ranger. Maybe some young buck gets his first coup tonight by sparing us?"

"Or his first scalp?"

"Either way, you wouldn't want to stand in the way of a man becoming a brave. Would

you?"

"Well since you put it that way. Maybe we should've shaved our heads. Who wants a bald scalp?"

"No, then it's worse. If you aren't worth scalping, they find an anthill and bury you up to your neck next to it. Then they cut off your eyelids so as to fully appreciate that desert sun."

"That's quite thoughtful."

His voice got serious. "Mr. Dumas, we're being stopped. Calm now, calm."

Three burly braves stopped us. Their tones were harsh and their glares fierce. The captain's voice was even keeled, and he spoke their tongue. I thought I heard my moniker. They patted us down for weapons and then just stared at us. After an eternity, one of the braves left.

An old woman came out, tossed a buffalo robe on the ground, and left into the darkness. The two braves bade us sit. Eventually we could see a hobblin' man bein' led to us.

"That'll be Ten Bears," whispered the captain. "Let me do the talking."

He was scarred and ancient, yet he had eyes that looked right through you. He had the silent aura of authority the military calls command presence. His guards stood to either side as we rose to meet him.

"It's been many seasons, Ten Bears."

"You are brave to come here, Dalton."

"Have I not smoked the peace pipe with Ten Bears, Chief of the Yamparika Comanche?"

Vestiges of a smile slowly cracked through the chief's weathered visage.

"True.... Yet Dalton lies now?"

"No."

"You tell my braves Dalton and *Fusil Largo* come to talk with Ten Bears."

"Yes."

"*Fusil Largo* has killed many braves from afar. This young one is not him."

"Look in his eyes."

Ten Bears grabbed me by the shoulders and stared through my soul.

"Old eyes, young one. You are *Fusil Largo*?"

"Yes."

He smiled a wolf smile with those mesmerizin' old dark orbs in his skull.

"It is possible. Your scalp would be a great honor for the Yamparika. We have smoked the peace pipe with Dalton, not you."

I smiled back.

"He smiles at death, Dalton."

"No," I replied.

"No?"

"Chief Ten Bears wouldn't kill a good enemy who comes unarmed to talk of peace."

"If I was young again, *Fusil Largo*, we would make a great fight, you and I."

I nodded.

Ten Bears turned back to the captain.

"I know why you come."

"Red Wolf will break the peace."

"Four more went past the soldiers to join him last night."

"You want peace for your people. you know it's hopeless to keep fighting the bluecoat army."

"I am old, Dalton. Red Wolf and his braves are young with hot blood. Now they have

Spencers too."

"You know how this ends. Big war. Think of your people."

"Red Wolf is Kiowa clan. I am a Comanche chief."

"There are Comanche braves with Red Wolf."

"I cannot stop them. I remember what it was like when I was young."

"Times have changed. You had a chance. Now they have no chance. Even if Red Wolf had a thousand Spencers, there are too many whites to fight with endless guns. In the end, the Kiowa cannot win. They must live in peace or be destroyed. You are wise and know this is true. A great war here ends the Comanche as well."

"You.... You speak true, Dalton."

"Tell me where Red Wolf trades for guns. We'll do the rest. Let's save your people, my people and the Kiowas."

Ten Bears suddenly turned back to me.

"*Fusil Largo*, your young blood still runs hot. Tell your enemy the truth. What would you do?"

I took a deep breath.

"I fight for my people. I will do anything to keep their blood away from the cold of death."

"You would cut your own, not fight?"

"If some of my people bring death to the rest. Yes, I cut them."

"You are the *Fusil Largo*."

He nodded again.

'It's south of here, in a few days. A cabin near Bear Mountain."

"Thank you, Ten Bears. We go to end this. Keep the peace."

The Chief wasn't finished.

"Go find these white men, but do not kill Red Wolf's braves. I know my people. They are like a dry summer grass in hot winds. One spark will set our world on fire. If the bluecoats kill any Kiowa or Comanche, all here will rise to the warpath.... All here."

"It's that bad?"

"Every promise is broken to us. We are warriors, many say the young braves show honor and we should die fighting with honor."

"That's where we are?"

"I speak true."

"We'll come back and smoke the peace pipe again."

"If you come back."

"Yes. If we come back."

ᴗᴗᴗᴗᴗᴗᴗ

We rode hard for Fort Worth. Indians were the army's responsibility and Major Duvall was seasoned and levelheaded.

There was only one problem.

Time was of the essence, and he wasn't there.

Lieutenant Ellis was sitting at the major's desk when we were ushered in.

"It's good to see you both again. We weren't sure to see you breathing again."

"Thank you. Where's Major Duvall?"

"He was ordered to Fort Sill for a few days, I'm in command until his return. What did you learn?"

"We know where Red Wolf meets the gun runners."

"Excellent! We can set an ambush for both Red Wolf and the gun runners. Wipe the slate clean."

"It's not that simple."

"Of course it is. This is an army matter. Where do they meet?"

"No, it's not."

"Why?"

"Ten Bears is wise and knows his people."

"This doesn't concern the reservation."

"His people are frustrated and divided. He stressed to us stop the gun runners, but if Red Wolf or his braves are killed, there will be an uprising."

"There is already an uprising."

I was losing patience with this buffoon.

I interjected, "Yes, so far it's thirty braves. What happens when over a thousand battle-hardened Comanche hit Dallas, Fort Worth, or any other spot on the map.... That's half the population of Dallas."

"He's bluffing."

Captain Dalton replied, "Ten Bears is trying to save his people. This is no bluff."

"If the hostiles rise up the army will crush them."

I asked, "Are you lookin' to make history, Lieutenant Ellis? What happens when a thousand Comanches kill, scalp, and rape Dallas on your watch?"

"The cavalry will crush them if they break the treaty."

"At least General Santa Anna would smile."

"Why would the Mexicans care?"

"Because if you bungle this, he'll be off the hook for Goliad and the Alamo, the largest massacres in Texas history."

He was glarin' at me now.

Ellis meant well. He was just dense.

"Where do they meet?"

"We forgot."

"You must tell me. This is army business... That's an order."

"We aren't under your command. Good afternoon, sir."

ᴜᴜᴜᴜᴜᴜᴜ

Ellis was partially right. Indian problems belonged to the Army. Renegade white gun runners were different. We sent Alligator back to help the marshal watch over Dallas, then rode west. At nightfall we turned south in a small stream. We rode hard for Bear Mountain and reached it the followin' mornin'.

The cabin wasn't much to speak of, just an old, whitewashed shack. There was also a small barn with rottin' walls out back.

Both were empty.

We put our horses up and settled down to wait.

"Captain, what happens if Red Wolf's raiders show up first?"

"That's a problem."

"What would we do?"

"We can't shoot them. Have you ever considered joining the Comanche Nation?"

"We could do worse."

"Let's have coffee and think on it."

It was a long lazy day until an hour before sunset.

Then we heard it.

Horses from the east.

We hid in the barn and waited. It was two bearded riders followed by a fat man on a mule-driven covered wagon.

The captain whispered, "These aren't choir boys and there may be more. Let's bust them fast."

I knelt, scooped up a handful of soil and let it slide through my fingers.

Ashes to ashes. Dust to dust.

"Mr. Dumas, I get a chill every time you do that."

"Yes, sir. Let me hit them from the side of the barn. Can you distract them toward the barn door?"

"Why don't we..."

"Trust me, sir."

He smiled and nodded.

I checked the action on my Henry and slipped out the back of the barn. I crept with my back along the side wall until I was braced just behind the corner.

My eyes closed and I imagined where they would be in my mind's eye. I took a deep breath, let half out, and waited for the signal as the wagon stopped out front.

One of them said, "Jerry, get them horses in the barn."

Then I heard clangin' from inside the door.

I came around the corner with the Henry spittin' fire.

A lever gun up close is lethal.

The closest of them was about eight yards away, then one beyond and behind him, and finally fatty on the wagon.

Skipper'd taught me boardin' house rules for multiple targets. Everyone gets a helpin' first, then seconds, or thirds, if you know what I mean...

I took them left to right as the barn door opened.

My first shot took the closest one just above the ear like an axe splittin' kindlin' in a crimson spray. He dropped like a poleaxed steer. The second renegade was turnin' toward me with his pistol when my second round took him in the stomach. He fell to his knees screamin' in disbelief at the blood suddenly seepin' through his shirt.

I sidestepped, then shot again.

Shoot then move, never both at once.

The third shot caught the big one on the wagon by the throat. He slumped forward droppin' the reins and fell off the wagon. I sidestepped and fired back into the kneelin' second one. His face exploded in a scream of dust and gore.

I was trackin' back for the prone one by the wagon when Captain Dalton waved me off.

"Lordy, that was smooth. They didn't even get a shot off."

I shrugged.

His eyes swept across the bodies, then he stared at me shakin' his head.

"What?"

"I don't want you comin' after me when I go rogue and quit the rangers for the big money robbing banks."

"That'll be the day."

The man from the wagon stirred on his belly with a moan. The captain kicked his pistol away and turned him over. We stood over him as dark blood gurgled from his mouth.

"Who.... Who are you?" he gasped.

"Texas Rangers."

"I'm dying..."

"Is that wagon full of rifles?"

He smiled wickedly through tobacco-stained teeth.

"We come from Oklahoma, but that ain't gonna help you none…Them Injuns ain't never late when out of bullets." He wheezed blood. "Wish I could see them scalp you."

"You won't see anything."

"See you in Hell."

"You first."

The captain put him out of his misery with a shot to the forehead.

It wasn't five minutes before we saw dust risin' on the horizon from up north.

"That'll be Red Wolf."

"Let's get the wagon in the barn."

"No time."

"Do we run for it?"

"No, we can't fight, or it starts a war. It's too late to run."

"Destroy the rifles?"

"No time for fire."

"What if I hold them off while you get the wagon in the barn and fire it?"

"Shane, there's at least thirty of them, and we can't kill."

"Yeah."

A pair of Kiowa scouts came over the rise.

We were the walkin' dead.

Then came the sweetest sound of luck possible.

A bugle blastin' out the cavalry charge from the east.

It's real.

Captain Dalton and I locked eyes in relieved disbelief.

The Kiowa scouts vanished in a blink.

I let out a deep breath and a tired smile.

"You should quit this rangerin' business, Shane."

"You think so?"

It's hard to explain the euphoria you feel when you know you're dead meat and then something saves you.

The air tastes sweet.

A warm wave of relief floods through your veins, and you feel incredibly hungry.

"If we were cats, we just lost a life." He grinned.

Sometimes the difference between life and death is that fast.

I looked east. "Lieutenant Ellis isn't movin' so fast."

"It doesn't matter if he crawls in, those Kiowa are halfway to Canada by now. This is over."

"Is it?"

"That renegade told us Red Wolf's out of ammo. His braves will desert him."

"I see."

"I never thought I'd be thrilled to see Lieutenant Ellis. It's a good thing he isn't as useless as tits on a bull and tracked us down."

"Sir?"

"Yes."

"What about justice for the Eklunds? Red Wolf just walks?"

"Yes. To stop a war. Yes."

"Yeah."

"Pete would understand. He was a ranger."

"You're right, sir."

"I don't like it either. That's the way the world is."

"Yeah."

"That was one close shave. I could actually kiss Lieutenant Ellis when he gets here."

"Maybe wash up first, so he doesn't arrest us again."

CHAPTER FIVE
COMANCHE WHISPERS

"There is nothing as eloquent as a rattlesnake's tail."
— **Navajo Proverb**

A week later

"DALLAS SEEMS DIFFERENT, MR. Dumas."

"We've only been gone a week, sir."

"Seems like a decade to me. The streets are so quiet."

"I could use a bath, a whiskey, and some enchiladas."

"In that order?"

"Not necessarily."

He laughed. "I'll meet you at the Yellow Rose in a few."

We met there after puttin' our horses up. The Yellow Rose had the best enchiladas in Dallas. Miss Laura, a handsome gray-haired woman with a colorful past, owned the saloon.

"Good afternoon, Shane."

"Hello, Miss Laura."

"Are you still engaged, young man?" She smiled crinklin' her nose. "Just checking."

I laughed. "Yes ma'am."

"All the good ones."

"Where's the usual supper crowd?"

She rolled her eyes. 'You'll see."

Captain Dalton ambled in, and we took down half a bottle of whiskey and a whole mess of enchiladas.

"I'm fixin' to take a proper bath and hit the sheets."

He shook his head. "I'm not so lucky."

"Oh?"

"Alligator and I have to testify against those rustlers in Nacogdoches."

"Now?"

"Yeah, we'll be gone a week or so. Are you off surveying this week?"

"No, I'll be in the office."

"Can you do me a favor, keep your badge on, and help the marshal keep an eye on things?"

Marshal Irvin was a local legend but gettin' a bit long in the tooth.

"Not a problem, sir."

Miss Laura brought us two more drinks. "Compliments of those fellows sitting by the window."

We raised out glasses to them in thanks.

One responded. "Great to have you rangers back in town."

Captain Dalton shrugged. "Well, that's mighty neighborly."

"Yup. Something does seem off though."

We sipped our second whiskeys and he paused, lookin' at his glass then me.

"If I recall, I saw a young fellow order a whiskey at Elroy's in Nacogdoches a few years back. Samson, the local bully, knocked the drink off the bar and pulled a knife on him. Big mistake. That young fellow drew in a blink and killed Samson with one shot to the chest."

"I didn't even sip a drink that night."

"Have you been to Elroy's since?"

"It's not my favorite place."

"I can see why."

"That sort of thing doesn't happen much anymore."

He laughed and insisted on payin' the tab. "That doesn't surprise me."

We shook, and off he went.

UUUUUUUU

I needed ammo for the Henry and made my way to Green's general store. The proprietor was a nice old gent from Kentucky who could sell snow in Canada.

"Mr. Dumas, it's certainly good to see you back."

"Well, thank you, Mr. Green."

"Yes sir, you're truly a sight for sore eyes."

"I laughed. "C'mon now. I'd like a couple of boxes of .44s."

"Oh, you're loading up too. I guess you've already heard?"

"What?"

"I only have a single box of .44 left. Yes sir, I sold more ammunition the last two days than I usually do in a month. I'm nearly dry."

"Is that so?"

"I'd have saved a bunch for you if I'd have known."

"Known what exactly?"

"You know, about the Comanches."

'Yeah, the Eklunds will be missed."

"Is the marshal calling a meeting?"

"Mr. Green, what are you talking about?"

"You ain't heard?"

"Heard what?"

"About the savages."

"Savages?"

"The Comanches."

"They're fixing to attack tomorrow! Today is the last day we've got to get ready for them.

That's why everybody's been hoping you'd be back in time. We have to get organized!"

"Where are they, Mr. Green?"

"Who?"

"The Comanches."

"I'm guessing they're out on a prairie somewhere. Now, what's our plan?"

"We don't have any plans."

"All righty, let me know. I can fight too. We've got womenfolk and youngsters to protect!"

"I have a question, Mr. Green."

"Shoot."

"How do you know the Comanches are set to raid Dallas tomorrow?"

"Everybody knows about it. That's why everyone's been buying up ammunition, getting ready."

"Who told everyone about the Comanches?"

"Just ask anybody. It's general knowledge."

"Is the whole town as jittery as you are?"

"I ain't jittery...This is serious. Them Comanche could destroy Dallas if there's enough of them."

"Yeah.... How many are there?"

"I don't know how many, a good-sized war party, I'm sure."

"Has anybody seen them?"

"No, not yet."

"It's tomorrow they're raidin' us? Well, I'll put the .44s on my bill, Mr. Green."

"...Uh would you mind paying cash, no offense."

"Serious?"

"I'm sorry. You being a ranger, always in the thick of the fighting, and all. No offense."

"All right." I forked over the coins.

"Let me know when plans are made, I'll tell everybody you're back and we'll have a meeting."

"No. Please wait till you hear from me, Mr. Green."

I spied Doc Parrish just outside the store on the street and left.

"Hello, Doc."

"Oh, hi, Shannon."

"Doc, I've just been talking to Mr. Green."

"Yes?"

"Is he gettin' soft in the head?"

"Oh, he must have told you about the Comanches."

"Yeah."

"Dallas is ablaze talking about it. Comanches are on the war path, they say,

and they're going to attack Dallas tomorrow, I believe it is."

"When did all this talk begin?"

"A few days back. Everybody's been right excited. Especially Green and Frank Reed at the Dallas house. They hoped the rangers would be back in time. What do you think?"

"Nothing."

"Well, everybody seems pretty certain about it."

"Who started all this talk, Doc?"

"Good question. Some drunk probably, or some greenhorn. Gossip spreads, and pretty soon everybody takes it for a fact, and then folks panic."

"Has anybody seen them?"

Well, everyone knows they hit the Eklund place, you might have a hard time talking folks down."

"Yeah. The Eklund business was rough."

"Did the raiders get justice?"

"We didn't catch them, but it's likely been dealt with. Did Alligator say somethin' about Comanches? Is that what this is?"

"I didn't even know he was back, but it's good to have you and Captain Dalton back. Where are Alligator, Snake and the rest of the rangers?"

"Most of them are still out after those rustlers. I'll see what Marshal Irvin thinks."

"It's better you didn't. I was just with him, and his consumption is flaring up. At his age, he needs a few days bedrest. It seems you are the only badge in Dallas for now."

"I see... Well, a Comanche raid would at least be good for your practice, Doc?"

He smiled. "I don't need that kind of business, maybe ask Miss Laura at the Yellow Rose. Nothing happens in Dallas without her knowing."

"Fair point, I was there for supper. It was surprisingly empty. Excuse me, Doc."

I made my way back to the Yellow Rose.

"Hello, Miss Laura."

"Back so soon? You go away for a whole week, and you come back with nothing but a big frown. What are you on the prod about?"

"Did anyone warn of a Comanche attack in here?"

"Oh, that. Here I was hoping you finally get the merits of an older woman." She grinned.

"How come you're not armed, Miss Laura?"

"Armed?"

"You're just going to let the Comanches ride off with you? Aren't you going to struggle a little?"

"Kind of exciting, isn't it, Shane?"

"You don't seem very worried."

"Why should I be? ... Dallas is full of heroes these days."

She gave a sly sideways glance at a long-haired old man at the end of the bar.

I laughed out loud. "Miss Laura, clearly I never gave you enough credit."

"For what?"

"You got proper sarcasm, to go with your looks."

"Don't tease an old widow, Shane." She smirked. "It's cruel.... Well, at least your smile's back. You need a beer?"

"No thanks, who's that at the end of the bar?"

"He's a sight, isn't he?"

"Buckskin-clad men are rare these days."

"His name's Jeremiah. He's at least eighty, and probably hasn't bathed this decade."

"A man his age has seen a lot of life, Miss Laura."

The old fellow finished his drink and left the saloon.

"Never mind him. What are you going to do about the Comanche, Shane?"

"I'll try to keep the good citizens of Dallas from getting all triggered up and shooting each other for Comanches these days."

"How?"

"I'd like to know who started all this, for one."

"Are Comanche braves as handsome as they say, Shane?"

"They definitely have sand to them."

"You'd be shocked if they really did raid this place, wouldn't you?"

"Yes, I would, but don't lose that scattergun you keep behind the bar."

"Shane, I hate sending anyone to the Dallas House, but maybe Charlie Pratt can help?"

I thanked her and headed for the Dallas House. Charlie Pratt tended bar at the Dallas House. He'd courted Miss Laura for a spell then lost interest, or so the story goes. He was a bald, noisy man with a hooked nose. I ordered a whiskey at the bar. When

I asked about the Comanche talk, he just shrugged and pointed at the end of the bar.

It was the same old man who'd just been drinkin' at the Yellow Rose. He limped over to me and smelled like a distillery.

"Ranger, are you? I'm Jeremiah. I want to offer my services."

I shook his hand. "Your services?"

He responded with a rabid dog rant. "There ain't nothing I don't know about Indians, young man. I scouted for Kit Carson. That was Apache over in New Mexico. Then there was the Skunk River fight in '48. It was Arapahos that time. I know Comanches inside and out,

backwards and forwards, dead and alive, chiefs and braves, squaws and papooses. I knows them all!"

"Well, that's fine, Mr. Jeremiah, but I don't think we've got anything to worry about."

"You can't trust an Indian, any more than you can trust a white man. They've all got sharp tongues and evil ways."

I hoped a beer would shut him up.

Charlie saw the business opportunity.

"Buy him a drink, Shane. That shuts the old devil up."

"All right, Charlie, please get him a beer."

"Well, thank you but beer is for womenfolk."

"Oh?"

"Straight whiskey sweetens my tobacco."

"Another whiskey please, Charlie."

He glared at Charlie. "Old devil, am I? Dallas will be grateful I'm here when them war ponies come screaming out of the dawn. Don't ever let Comanche take you alive.... I've seen them spread eagle a man and..."

Charlie sneered. "Drink it and get out."

He faced me again. "Let me know when you need me. You fight Indians by attacking first. They're crazy, wild, and savage."

"Mr. Jeremiah, where did you hear about this Comanche raid?"

"Everybody's heard about it. Lock the women and children in the church, young Ranger. Leave them enough guns to shoot themselves, if worse comes to worse. There may not be enough real Indian fighters around here to hold off them bloodthirsty red men!"

"Who told you about the raid, Mr. Jeremiah?"

"When's the meeting?"

"Well, I don't know, but I expect that'll soon be common knowledge, too."

"Thanks for the drink."

He gulped his shot and staggered out the bar. I could see a crowd formin' outside the Marshal's office. The local hothead, Frank Reed, was gesticulatin' to a gaspin' crowd like the pope hisself. I headed over to them.

"It's about time we saw some law step up!" Frank Reed yelled out. "Where's Captain Dalton and the Marshal?"

"I reckon this is the organizing committee, huh?"

"Someone got to do something to keep Dallas safe!”

“Mr. Reed, I don’t recall you volunteerin’ for the posse after the Eklund raid.”

A lady from the crowd gasped. “What’s the plan, to keep us safe?”

I raised my arms for attention and addressed the crowd.

“Folks, these Comanche rumors are needlessly spookin’ Dallas.”

The crowd replied with jeers, curses, and agitation.

Old Jeremiah stepped out of the crowd. “This ranger is too young to know. They always attack at dawn. The Comanches are the bloodiest devils in the whole Indian nation...Why...they...”

I cut him off.

“Who here heard about the Comanche raid first?”

A man in the crowd yelled, “Does it matter? We don’t have much time. Why, my wife's nearly crazy with fear, all the womenfolk are. We got to do something, get organized...While there’s still time!”

“All right Mr. Jeremiah, one question.”

“Now, we’re getting somewhere.”

“In all your experience, have you ever known the Comanche to let a town know exactly when they’re goin’ to strike?”

This quieted their fervor but only for a bit.

Frank Reed yelled back, "What if you're wrong? They'll be here at dawn. It's your job as the law here to protect Dallas. If you don't help us now, the blood will be on your head!"

"Blood?" I raised my voice. "Do you all know what panic is? It's when people stop thinkin'."

A man in the crowd replied, "That's strong talk, Ranger. What if you're wrong?"

"Is it? Consider this, say the Comanche are on the warpath and comin' at dawn. Why is it no one knows of this knowledge? Mr. Jeremiah, you never answered my question."

He screamed hysterically, "They're downright mean! I know them."

"Answer the question, sir."

They're just like snakes. They never tell nobody nothing. It's just a whoosh then you got an arrow right in your throat."

"The only person who would know would be a Comanche. Folks, has anyone seen Comanche braves in town lately getting drunk in the saloons?...Well?"

The old timer's voice cracked in derangement. "They are coming, fools! You'll all be sorry you didn't listen."

I could see eyes in the crowd registerin' his hysteria.

"Mr. Jeremiah, no more wild Comanche talk out of you, please. The rest of you please go on home and calm down your womenfolk. I'll spend nights in the marshal's office until he's back on his feet."

The crowd slowly calmed down with a wave of murmurs. A voice from the back said, "He's right, it sure don't seem right if you stop to think on it."

Mr. Jeremiah wasn't finished. "It's a free country. The law don't muzzle a man in America!"

"Sir, when did you hit Dallas?"

"A few days back, why?"

"I believe your wild talk started all of this. If you continue to disturb the peace, I'll throw you in jail until you sober up. Now please behave, sir."

ՍՍՍՍՍՍՍ

It's impossible to sleep right in jail. Poundin' on the door woke me well before dawn. Charlie Pratt was near a state of panic.

"Good mornin', Mr. Pratt."

"You slept dressed?"

"I figured there might be trouble yet."

'The Comanches set fire to the Davis rooming house."

"What? That's in town."

"How do we know it was Indians?"

"There were arrows nearby. It's bad, two dead."

"Who? Shot two dead and scalped?"

"I don't know."

"Let's go."

∪∪∪∪∪∪∪

Frank Reed and the crows were fumin' at the embers of the Davis House. He was practically foamin' at the mouth playin' the crowd once more. The Davis house wasn't much more than a shack drunks or cowpokes who'd been cleaned out at cards used.

It was Mr. Davis himself who found the arrows.

"Who was killed? Were they shot and scalped?"

"We don't know. Two charred bodies were found inside, Drunks or drifters likely. We found the arrows sticking in the ground out back."

"That settles it!" Frank Reed said. "It's war! Let's get the army after them. These savages need to die!"

"Everyone calm down," I replied. "Why would they only burn this one house?"

"We've listened to you long enough. What more proof do you need? We have women to protect! Let's kill them all! Hit them first, I say!"

The crowd was on the cusp of turnin' into a mob.

Then it hit me.

Old Jeremiah was surprisingly silent and lurkin' at the edge of the crowd for his moment of triumph. He saw me starin' and drifted off into town.

I yelled to the crowd. "If this proves Jeremiah right, why did the great Indian fighter slink away when I arrived?"

No one had an answer for that.

"Look smoke at the livery house!" someone yelled out.

All eyes turned as one in that direction and rushed for the livery stables.

Old Doc Parrish came limpin' out the side with his medical bag in hand.

Folks rushed over to him.

"Are you hurt, Doc? Did you see Comanche?"

"There's no fire." Doc shook his head irritably and raised his voice. "Has anyone seen old Jeremiah?"

"Maybe the savages got him!" a lady from the crowd screeched. "God bless his soul!"

Doc raised his hands and yelled for attention.

"Everyone listen to me! ...Everyone, I was comin' to help when I saw Mr. Jeremiah tryin' to set kindlin' behind the horse stables. He gave me the slip."

"Jeremiah was fixin' to fire the livery?"

"The ranger was right!"

"Let's hang that old devil!"

"Yeah, let's find a tall tree!"

Now the mob realizin' they'd been taken was truly gettin' ugly.

I fired my Colt into the sky.

"Everyone relax. First, we let an old fool panic us. Now we want his blood for believin' him?"

"Two men are dead from his fire!"

"Yes, there's hell to pay."

"We need justice."

"Mr. Jeremiah will hang if guilty, but first he gets a fair trial.... I'll sort this out."

"What if he gets away?" Frank Reed exclaimed.

"Mr. Reed, do you truly believe I can't track down an eighty-year-old man on foot?"

∪∪∪∪∪∪∪∪

I rode him down about a mile outside of Dallas. He was wild-eyed and incoherent.

When I told him his little stunt had killed two men he was dazed and said somethin' to the effect it was no big loss, that white men were devils too and couldn't be trusted. Then he started cryin', begged for a drink, and passed out from the heat.

He didn't say a word for the next three days as peace returned to Dallas. Marshal Irvin succumbed to the consumption and was buried the followin' day. Unfortunately, I couldn't risk leavin' the jail for the service. Captain Dalton still wasn't back, and I had to guard him close since the locals were still ashamed of their panic, and truly wanted to lynch him for it.

The Comanches actually showed up a day after Captain Dalton's return.

One single Comanche.

An Indian woman rode right into Dallas in broad daylight and stopped at the jail.

She asked for me of all people and I was fetched to the marshal's office. The woman was middle aged and handsome, and carried herself with the instinctive dignity of a warrior people. I admired her courage ridin' into Dallas alone like that.

"I am Blue Flower of the Yamparika. Are you *Fusil Largo*?"

"Yes ma'am."

"Ten Bears sends me to invite you and Dalton to smoke the peace pipe."

"I am, and we will. Why do you ask for me?"

"There is more. You have brought an old man in jail here. He is also Yamparika, Ten Bears sends me to bring him home."

"Mr. Jeremiah lived among the Comanche? How do you know I brought him to jail?"

She smiled. "We see all in our lands."

"That seems to be the case."

"Jeremiah is my father. He's always been trouble."

"That explains your English?"

"Yes."

"He's still in trouble. He set a fire and two men were killed."

"His mind is broken. He drinks too much, gets mad, and angers all. He made strong war talk and Ten Bears sent him away."

"I see. It's not that simple. A judge here will decide his fate. If he's found guilty, he may hang."

"Release him to me. We will give horses in payment."

"A judge must rule on him first."

"May I speak to this judge for my father?"

Captain Dalton spoke up. "I don't see why not, but it might not help. We can at least let you talk with your father."

The trial lasted a single day. Dallas needed to get past this mess, elect a new marshal, and truth be told free up that jail cell. Judge Thiel expedited things.

Mr. Jeremiah babbled incoherently in Comanche on the stand. Blue Flower spoke of her father and said he was always a harmless fool, but his mind shattered in grief after her mother passed. She said he was just a crazy old drunk, promised he would never be trouble to Dallas again, and begged to take him home. For what it was worth I also testified I felt his mind was gone, and asked at his age what good does jail do?

However, I think Captain Dalton's ever pragmatic rationale sealed it. He told the judge, this old fool was one of Ten Bear's people, and told him how we all owed Ten Bears for helpin' stop the gun runnin' that could have set the frontier on fire. He said the Christian thing was to release this old fool to his kin, or if you were a cynic, let the Comanches handle the Jeremiah problem.

I don't think Jeremiah knew what all the fuss was about or even cared. After seeing his daughter, he spoke only in Comanche from that point. Judge Thiel gave Blue Flower a stern warning that Jeremiah would be hung on sight if he ever set foot in Dallas again.

Then he released Jeremiah to her custody.

At the edge of town, I said goodbye and watched them ride off into the sunset, both mounted on her pony. The old man, chattering like a bird, happy to be going home.

No longer lonely under that vast, blue Texas sky.

CHAPTER SIX
ROBIN

"Our first teacher is our own heart."

– Cheyenne Proverb

Two weeks later

"MARSHAL DUMAS HAS A certain ring to it."

"No chance, sir."

Captain Dalton's belly laugh filled the saloon. "I'm just saying the position is vacant."

"I agree," Alligator added.

I was blurry eyed after countless whiskeys.

"You agree he'd make a good marshal, or no chance?"

"Both," the big man said. "Shane would make a better preacher."

"You are both miles off the reservation."

"You handled Dallas quite well with that Jeremiah affair."

"Thanks but preachin' isn't for me. I'm not patient enough for church on Sundays, and I don't think my stomach could handle the constant obligatory fried chicken dinners from well-meanin' but poor cooks in the congregation."

Alligator fell off his stool laughin'. "So true."

"If Dallas is home, I don't mind pitchin' in and doin' my part against raiders and bad men some, but the law isn't a good profession for a family man. I'm goin' to marry René at Christmas, run that ranch, and raise a mess of kids."

"Yeah." The captain nodded. "That's a good life."

There was an envelope on the table. Captain Dalton spilled a bit of water on it and scooped it to the side.

"Oh, I suppose that's a hint I should go deal with this."

"What's in it?"

"It's from the War Department. It says proceed to Fort Worth and receive return prisoners from Major Duvall."

"The War Department?"

"Yes, we are to hold them in Dallas until the arrival of a Mr. Randal Parker of Boston."

"Why task us with army business?"

"Well, as usual, the government doesn't explain much."

"Fort Worth is a full thirty-mile ride from here, and how many prisoners?"

"It doesn't say."

"Sir, there could be half a dozen of them. I'll come with."

"I appreciate it. Shane, we'll leave at dawn. The next round is on me, boys."

ՍՍՍՍՍՍՍՍ

"Good afternoon, boys. Hasn't soap been discovered in Dallas?"

"We wanted to remind the army what real fighting men look and smell like." Captain Dalton smirked.

Major Duvall belly laughed. "I should have the good lieutenant throw you two back in the brig. Officer quarters aren't luxurious here, but we'll find a spot for you. When will you start back to Dallas?"

"Dawn, if the prisoners are ready."

"Prisoners?"

"Is there some sort of mix-up again?"

"That's the only description they gave?"

"Yes. Hold returned prisoners in Dallas for a gentleman from Boston. Whatever 'returned prisoners' means."

"The prisoner was a captive of the Comanche and returned to us several weeks ago."

"Oh."

"Why not keep him at Fort Worth or just send him home?"

"It's a woman. Mrs. Judith Parker was captured, on a stagecoach, while traveling to join her husband in Santa Fe ten years ago. She was the sole survivor. The man who's coming out from Boston for her is her husband."

"Ten years is a long time for a woman to live with Indians."

"It takes time coming from Boston. They figured it best she waits in Dallas."

"Since when is sending a woman to Dallas a safer option?"

"Orders are orders."

I asked, "How did she escape?"

"She won't talk about it. We had a squadron chasing Chief Santa Anna's band a few weeks back and they came across Mrs. Parker and a girl out on the plains."

"A girl?"

"A Comanche, not a white girl."

"I see."

"Washington has decided she goes home, and they send the girl to a reservation."

"Fair enough."

"It's going to take a little time to sort this all out. Mrs. Parker absolutely refuses to be separated from the girl."

"So, for now we escort them both to Dallas?"

"Precisely."

I asked, "How old is the girl?"

"I reckon eight to twelve."

"We'll introduce ourselves at supper."

"No, Mrs. Parker insists on eating alone with the girl and they're both still in Indian robes."

"I'm sure this will go over good and smooth. Major, do you have a bottle of proper rye hidden in this office?"

"Sir, yes sir."

ᴗᴗᴗᴗᴗᴗᴗ

Major Duvall introduced us the followin' mornin'. "Mrs. Parker, this is Captain Dalton, and Mr. Dumas of the Texas Rangers. They will escort you to Dallas and take care of things until your husband arrives."

Mrs. Parker was a handsome woman, with a jagged scar below her left eye, and an aura of quiet strength to her. I suppose that made sense given what she'd endured.

She asked with a worried look, "You'll take both of us?"

"Yes ma'am." The captain smiled. "It's a pleasure to meet you both. Perhaps the army can spare a wagon."

"Thank you, gentlemen. A wagon won't be necessary."

"It's thirty miles to Dallas, ma'am."

She smiled. "We have Comanche ponies and have made longer trips."

I nodded. "Come to think of it that makes perfect sense, ma'am."

"Are you from back east, Mr. Dumas?"

"New Orleans, ma'am."

"I can still hear the accent."

The captain asked, "Does the girl speak English?"

"A little, but don't expect her to talk, she's frightened of white men. Her name is Robin."

The captain tipped his hat. "It's nice to meet you, Robin."

I added. "Ma'am, please tell her, my name is Shannon, we are friends and will protect both of you."

Robin smiled faintly then looked down again.

"Thank you. She understood but thank you."

We got started and didn't talk much for the first few hours. It was clear both of them were expert riders.

Around noon, the captain asked, "Mrs. Parker, we often chase raiders, may I ask your opinion on a tough subject?"

She nodded.

"Ma'am, if there are female captives, we push real hard the first few days. Do you think this helps overall or puts captives in greater danger?"

She didn't hesitate. "It was hell in the beginning. If you are asking if it's a good idea to try to catch raiders before they get tired of raping us, the answer is yes. They try to make sure there is enough distance between them and any pursuers first. The third night was worst. The women are the real danger. If the men don't kill you at once, they'll take turns with you until the novelty wears off. The women...Well they are the ones who cut you, burn you, and such."

She tapped the scar on her face.

I was awed by her strength.

The lady was recountin' hell in the casual tone folks use when describin' a laundry list.

"Ma'am, sorry if we are distressing you?"

"No, it's fine." She looked us in the eye. "It's good you chase hard. Most don't survive the first week, but if you do you have a chance. I got very lucky, in hindsight. I had a baby at the time."

She looked away at the horizon.

"We can change the subject, ma'am."

"No, it's important folks know the Comanche respect strength above all. Their village was by a large pond. The men were sick of my baby's crying. They took him from me and threw him in the water. I dove in after him. This became a game. They kept throwing Steven back in and betting how many times I could save him."

Oh my god.

She continued. "After the fourth or fifth time I was exhausted. I got so mad I grabbed a fallen branch and decked the closest brave as hard as I could. I was sure they'd slit my throat, but they all fell over laughing. Chief Santa Anna liked my spirit, I guess. The abuse stopped then and there. He eventually made me one of his eight wives. Steven died of fever the following winter though."

"You are truly a brave soul, ma'am."

She shook her head. "Do you have children, Mr. Dumas?"

"No, ma'am. Someday, I hope."

"You'll understand, I'm not brave, when you do."

We didn't talk much for the rest of the ride.

ՍՍՍՍՍՍՍՍ

Dallas was bustlin' and loud on our arrival. Everyone stopped to stare at us. We could tell Robin was frightened and the captain gave her a fatherly pat on the shoulder.

"This is the Dallas house, Miss Parker. I'll go see if they have a room for you."

"Thank you, Captain."

The owner of the Dallas House, Jake Rathman, was good people.

I carried their bag in as the captain said, "They'll want a room here for maybe two weeks.

Jake smiled. "I need some guests in this place. Two weeks is fine."

I added, "Please give them your best room, Jake. They've had a rough ride."

"Of course!"

"Mrs. Parker, this is Jake Rathman. He owns the Dallas House."

A dark look came over Jake's face when he first saw them.

I said, "We'll get you some different clothes tomorrow, ma'am."

Jake was gruff. "Are you really a white woman?"

"What? Of course she is, Jake," the captain snapped irritably.

"What about the little squaw?"

"Robin is Comanche, but she's staying with Miss Parker."

"Not here she ain't."

"Listen Jake, Miss Parker was a Comanche captive for years. She escaped with this girl. They're exhausted and need lodging."

"The white lady can stay here, but I ain't taking in no filthy squaws."

I got in his face. "You should be ashamed."

"I ain't running no hotels for savages, or come to think of it, anyone dressed like them."

The captain growled, "Jake, I see you in church every Sunday. This is a good Christian woman taken by the Indians. She's endured Hell and survived. Where is your mercy?"

Jake roared back, "Mercy? Mercy. Have you forgotten what the Comanches did to Wilma Eklund? You, rangers never even caught those raiders. Hell, if there's any justice in this world that there dirty little squaw will get exactly what Mrs. Eklund..."

Captain Dalton knocked him out cold.

Jake hit the floor in a heap and the captain was red furious. I held him back from stompin' Jake until he calmed down.

"Captain, please. I'll handle it."

The captain stormed out of the hotel before he killed someone.

Mrs. Dalton and Robin were frozen in silence. The girl was in her mother's arms.

I checked that Jake was breathin' and doused him with a bucket of water.

He came to, took a knee and began rubbin' his jaw.

"That was a cheap shot." He glared. "This is my hotel."

"Feel free to go finish it with the captain then. I was wrong to think so highly of you, Jake. You hate the Comanche so much? You want to fight them? The Comanche are brutal because they're facin' the end of their civilization. What's your excuse? Why do you threaten young girls instead of volunteerin' for a posse or the rangers? Are you scared of fightin' grown men?"

"Get out of my establishment."

"I apologize for him, Mrs. Parker."

"Can we just leave, Mr. Dumas? It's not going to work in Dallas."

"Please take Robin outside, ma'am. I'll be right behind you."

Once they'd left, I stared Jake Rathman in the eyes.

"You got a big mouth, Jake. If anyone bothers Mrs. Parker or Robin I'm comin' for you, and there will be blood."

In hindsight we should have taken them to the Yellow Rose from the get-go. Miss Laura had a few rooms out back and her heart melted at their tale. She welcomed them warmly and assured me they could stay as long as needed.

Captain Dalton and I got them situated and thankfully Robin' had stopped shakin'.

"Thank you both, but there will just be more trouble. I was naïve to think otherwise."

"Ma'am, nobody else will bother you. You escaped from the Comanche after all. Everything else is easy by comparison."

"We didn't escape. Robin and I were allowed to leave."

"I never heard of the Comanche doing that before?"

"It was Chief Santa Anna's decision."

"But why?"

"You may not understand it. but after the first few years, they treated me like one of the tribe. I still knew I could never be happy away from my own people."

"We are your people."

"What about Robin?"

"Robin?"

"He must have known she'd end up on a reservation."

"No, never!"

In hindsight, it was glaringly obvious. "Captain, Robin is Mrs. Parker's daughter."

"Yes! So, the reservation will not happen! Please don't tell anyone, I will tell Mr. Parker myself."

"Yes ma'am. Our lips are sealed. Let's see what we can sort out."

"I will not lose a second child."

"Understood, ma'am."

∪∪∪∪∪∪∪∪

Captain Dalton was called away the next day yet again. This time to deal with Mexican bandits. I volunteered to go. He asked me to stick around and watch over Mrs. Parker and Robin since they were familiar with me.

It was only a matter of days until Mr. Parker was due from Boston. Miss Laura told me Mrs. Parker and Robin demanded to work for their keep. She kept them back in the kitchen where no one would bother them. They didn't complain a lick, but I figured after three days cooped up in a kitchen maybe they'd like to go fishin'. They were up for it, and I told them I'd swing by the followin' mornin'.

That evenin' just before we closed shop, there was a knock at the office door. It was a large, bearded man with old, weathered eyes.

"Mister Dumas?"

"I'm George Hawkins and on my way to Oregon."

"We don't survey that far." I laughed.

He nodded. "May I talk to that woman, Mrs. Parker, you brought to Dallas?"

"Why?"

"I'll tell her that, sir."

"No, sir. What's your reason?"

He told me.

I heard him out and then told him to swing by the office at noon tomorrow.

The next day, I escorted Mrs. Parker and Robin to my office around noon. Miss Laura had packed us a picnic basket and Rob lent us his wagon and fishin' poles. She agreed to speak with Mr. Hawkins knowin' I'd be there.

He came in at noon, removed his hat, and smiled.

"It's a pleasure to meet you, ma'am. I'm George Hawkins."

"It's nice to meet you, sir."

He smiled at Robin. "Hello young lady. You sure take after your mother."

Mrs. Parker shook her head at me in short, formal, disappointment. "Mr. Dumas, how could you?"

"Ma'am, neither the captain nor I told a soul."

Mr. Hawkins interjected. "No one told me, ma'am. She has your eyes."

"I see." Mrs. Parker sighed. "If you see it, so will others. Shane, I'm so sorry..."

"All good, ma'am."

"What can I do for you, Mr. Hawkins?"

"Maybe you know something about my wife?"

"How's that?"

"Yes, ma'am. The Kiowas captured her about five years ago. There's a joint Kiowa and Comanche reservation at Red River, and I believe these two tribes often intermix. Her name is Jean."

"The Kiowas had a white woman once, blonde, captured on the Gila River. I never met her, though."

"Jean's a blonde, and that's where she was taken."

"Oh. Mr. Hawkins, when I heard of her, she'd already died. I'm sorry."

His eyes were downcast. Then he nodded slowly.

"Jean was never very strong. We should have stayed back east."

"It wasn't your fault, Mr. Hawkins. Things just go bad sometimes."

"I hope it wasn't too hard for you, ma'am."

"Life's not fair."

"I hope I haven't said anything to trouble you, ma'am."

"People talk, but they don't know. They got no idea what it was like."

"That's very true."

"Thank you for telling me what you knew."

He turned to leave. "Thank you, Mr. Dumas."

He turned slowly for the door, as if the weight of the world was on his shoulders.

Mrs. Parker asked, "Shane, did I count four fishing poles in the wagon?"

"Yes, ma'am."

"Shane, is it all right if Mr. Hawkins fishes with us a bit?"

He actually smiled. "I won't be any trouble, Mr. Dumas."

"I know. Let's go catch a mess of bass!"

My Skipper always told me there's nothin' like fishin' for the soul. It turned out to be a lovely afternoon. It makes sense in hindsight. Maybe it was the shared tragedy, or just good people. It felt like we weren't relative strangers.

As brutal as captivity must be, it might be worse to know a loved one is sufferin' it.

Regardless, we caught a mess of fish and at some point I caught a smile on all of them. At one point the three of us watched Robin gigglin' as she chased a slippery fish in the shallows.

"Thank you for this, Shane."

"My pleasure, ma'am."

We had pan-fried fish and coffee for supper.

On the wagon ride home, Robin fell asleep in her mother's lap.

Mr. Hawkins was sittin' up front with me.

"I'm grateful as well, Mr. Dumas."

"There's never a bad day fishin'."

ᴜᴜᴜᴜᴜᴜᴜ

Mr. Parker showed up the followin' afternoon. He was a small fidgety man in a dark blue suit.

"Mr. Dumas, I'm Randal Parker."

"Good mornin'."

"I've come for my wife."

"I'll take you to her."

He balked at the heat. "This is my first trip west since...Since Mrs. Parker was lost, in fact."

"Will you stay?"

"Heavens no, we'll go straight back to Boston...Uh, no offense."

"I'm from New Orleans myself."

"That's civilization too. Years ago we wanted land and freedom. We were fools."

"Mrs. Parker is fine, though I expect you'll see some changes in her."

"I expect as much. She's been through a terrible ordeal. I'll get her back to normal right quick."

"Your wife has grit, sir."

"She was a well-bred woman, I only hope she hasn't, well, lost too much."

I wasn't sure how to reply to that and led him to their rooms. I gave them some privacy but thought to stick around outside just in case he took the Robin news poorly. It would be hard on any man.

They came out yellin' about ten minutes later.

He glared at me. "It's all wrong. The squaw will go to the reservation where she belongs. This was arranged in Washington."

"No, Randal, over my dead body."

"Well, you can hardly expect me to take that girl back to Boston."

"It's up to you, I guess."

"Mr. Dumas, can you hold the squaw here in jail until we leave Dallas?"

"I'll do no such thing. Folks, please calm down."

"Randal. We lost one child. Robin is my daughter! I'll never leave her."

"She's not mine, I won't have her in my house."

"Then I'm sorry...Go back to Boston. I'll stay here."

"Do you know what you're saying?"

"Yes."

"I'll divorce you. You'll never get a red cent."

"I don't want your money."

"Fine, stay in Dallas. You're nothing better than an old squaw yourself now!"

I bit my tongue. "Excuse me, Mr. Parker."

"What do you want?"

"There's a train east leaving tonight."

"What's your point?"

"You're going to be on it, conscious or unconscious, either way."

"Are you threatening me?"

"Yes."

ԱԱԱԱԱԱԱ

The followin' mornin' I headed over to the Yellow Rose early and bought them breakfast. Robin didn't make a sound or touch her food. It was clear Mrs. Parker hadn't slept all night.

"Don't worry ma'am, we'll get the captain, Rob, Doc Parrish, and Miss Laura together and figure somethin' out. You are among friends."

She forced a smile, but it was clear the uncertainty was overwhelmin'. We looked up to see Mr. Hawkins walk in and remove his hat.

"May I sit?"

She nodded.

"Mrs. Parker, I understand your husband arrived and that he's left."

"Yes."

"What's next?"

"I don't rightly know. I will not give Robin up to a reservation. I could care less about Washington's orders."

"Maybe we should go fishing." He smiled.

"I'm not sure even fishing can fix this." She turned back to me. "Shane, do you think they will understand she's my daughter?"

"I honestly don't know, ma'am. Common sense says yes, but Washington's a long way away and can be obtusely rigid with orders. The captain and I were hopin' you'd be long gone by the time Washington followed up."

"So, it's best we clear out."

"We will figure it out, ma'am."

Mr. Hawkins took a deep breath. "I'm heading for Oregon, like I told you. I can leave any time. I got plenty of room for two more, like you and Robin."

"Do you really want us?"

His eyes were moist. "Well, I'll tell you…. I can't explain it. When we were talking and fishing, I felt I've known you my whole life…"

"Do you mean that?"

"I've only been waiting around Dallas to be certain you and Robin were going to be fine. Do you understand what…. I mean…What I'm trying to say, Mrs. Parker?"

She smiled for the first time. "Yes. Yes, I understand."

"It's settled then," Mr. Hawkins said.

"Shane, your René is one lucky girl." Mrs. Parker placed her hand in mine. "Will this be government trouble for you?"

"Texas is a big place, ma'am. Folks go missin' all the time." I smiled with a shrug and offered my hand to Mr. Hawkins. Mrs. Parker and Robin gave me bear hugs.

"Godspeed to you folks."

A cool wind gust, cut through the late summer heat. It was already September and summer was long in the tooth. I watched them board a train under the late afternoon sun.

Somehow, I knew they'd be just fine.

They had a chance at happiness.

It was their eyes.

They looked at each other the way a family does.

My Skipper and Miss Vivian had that same look back in New Orleans.

This was my Comanche summer. All of this made me miss René. I couldn't wait to hold her in my arms again and hear her laugh.

I was reminded of something Miss Vivian had once told me.

"If you have a chance for happiness, it's always worth the risk."

FIND ME ON SOCIALS

Did you enjoy **Comanche Summer?** This novelette features characters and adventures from the full-length Ballad of Shannon Dumas series.

<u>The Ballad of Shannon Dumas</u>
SHANNON

DODGE CITY

FATHER KING

And Coming Soon...
BLOOD DEBT

I'd like to invite you to join **"Wooden Nickels,"** my monthly newsletter! There are book extras, writing tips, contents, prizes, food for thought and the odd irresistible Tex-Mex recipe. It's also where I often seek your input on covers, character names,

A. K. VYAS

book titles, etc., and my list for new releases, special sales, and giveaways. **Join the fun.**

Website: akvyas.com

Facebook: @akvbook

Twitter: @akvyas18

Instagram: @akvyasauthor

ABOUT THE AUTHOR

A. K. VYAS GAVE early promise of being nothing special whatsoever. He was born in the small New England village best known for the witch trials, then banished to Texas at a tender age. Being annoyingly well read for a Texan and exceptionally stubborn as a child, the smart money predicted a brief but clumsy career as a rodeo clown, while others foresaw an early death.

To everyone's intense disbelief, UC Berkeley made the mistake of admitting him, and he squeaked out a degree or two while doing silly acrobatic things in small planes. The Navy eventually decided it was safer for all parties involved (including the enemy) if he didn't fly jets. Like most wayward souls he ended up on Wall Street, a lifestyle interrupted from time to time by an occasional date, unless of course it was NCAA football season. (You can take a boy out of Texas but can't take Texas out of the boy.)

To date, his young family has survived two Category 5 hurricanes, and an infatuation with Tex-Mex cast-iron skillet recipes. Europe is currently home, and for unknown reasons, people on the street everywhere always ask him for directions. *The Eagle Feather* was his debut attempt at the ancient art of storytelling, and was written for his beautiful, perfect, athletic, and wonderful young son.

Writing has since evolved into a cathartic hobby.

ALSO BY A.K. VYAS

The Eagle Feather Saga

The Eagle Feather Saga is the unforgettable story of one boy's perilous journey to lead his tribe amidst the daunting challenges and savage splendor of prehistoric times.

Texas Tales

Texas Tales is a series of Western short stories about the legendary wanderings of a lone cowboy you'll root for on the 19th Century Texas Frontier.

Carnival Girls

Carnival Girls is a dark international thriller about a chilling serial killer who abducts coeds and the FBI agent trying to bring him to justice.